The Promise (Pennington Family)

The Rebel

Secret Vows Box Set

Borrowed Dreams (Scottish Dream Trilogy Book 1)

Captured Dreams (Book 2)

Dreams of Destiny (Book 3)

Scottish Dream Trilogy Box Set

Romancing the Scot

It Happened in the Highlands

Sweet Home Highland Christmas

Sleepless in Scotland

Dearest Millie

How to Ditch a Duke

A Prince in the Pantry

Highland Crown (Royal Highlander Series Book 1)

Highland Jewel (Book 2)

Highland Sword (Book 3)

Ghost of the Thames

Thanksgiving in Connecticut

Made in Heaven

Marriage of Minds: Collaborative Writing

Step Write Up: Writing Exercises for 21st Century

———————

NOVELS BY NIK JAMES

Caleb Marlowe Westerns

High Country Justice

Bullets and Silver

Silver Trail Christmas

Henry Jordan Westerns

The Winter Road

NOVELS BY JAN COFFEY

Trust Me Once

Twice Burned

Triple Threat

Fourth Victim

Five in a Row

Silent Waters

Cross Wired

The Janus Effect

The Puppet Master

Blind Eye

Road Kill

Mercy

When the Mirror Cracks

Tropical Kiss

Aquarian

A PRINCE IN THE PANTRY

A REGENCY NOVELLA

MAY MCGOLDRICK

MM BOOKS

Thank you for choosing this book. In the event that you appreciate this book, please consider sharing the good word(s) by leaving a review, or connect with the author.

A Prince in the Pantry

Cover Art by Elefont Books Cover Design

1

———

London

May, 1814

Pearl Smith drew a handkerchief out of the cuff of her sleeve and patted the perspiration from her upper lip. The windowless sewing room in the basement of Londonderry House was suffocatingly hot.

The work on the cream-figured, silk muslin dress was finished. The garment hung on the wall hook, the hem mended. It was the only project that had been left for her today, and Pearl was glad. She was anxious to get back to her father, who was battling a summer cold and refused to take his dinner unless she was there with him.

Gathering up her bag and basket, she turned and started for the door but stopped short as she banged her knee on one of the benches.

She paused to rub the bruise, but it was quickly forgotten

when a screech from a child drew Pearl's head up. A consoling voice drifted in from the laundresses' room next door, along with the higher pitch of other children.

Every day, the women brought their youngsters—some infants, others barely waist high. Some helped and some sat or lay swaddled along a wall while the mothers worked. Whatever grievance Pearl had with the uncomfortable room she was assigned to do her sewing in, her situation was nothing compared to how those laundresses suffered. The heat and the steaming odors of soap and starch and bluing rising from the great wooden vats was dreadful. And that was before lugging their heavy baskets out into the bleaching and drying fields in Hyde Park.

In her previous life, Pearl had scarcely thought of how hard servants worked, but she now recognized the endless drudgery and discomfort these people endured.

The clock chimed the noon hour as she stepped out of the sewing room. Walking down the hallway, she was thinking of stops she needed to make when an upstairs maid suddenly appeared in her path.

"Sorry, miss. But are you leaving?"

"I've finished my work for the day. Why?"

"Begging your pardon, but the mistress sent me down for you. She wants you in her sitting room."

Pearl looked past the young woman down the corridor. She still had an hour of brisk walking to get home to her father.

The maid must have sensed her misgivings. "I can tell her you already left, if you like."

All of the servants were aware of Pearl's situation. It was no secret, and a few actually treated her with a mixture of sympathy and kindness. This woman was one of them.

Pearl laid a gentle hand on the woman's arm and shook her head. "It's all right. I'll go up and see Miss Cly before I leave."

The Londonderry House was the town residence of Lord Castlereagh, the Foreign Secretary. The powerful politician and his wife had no children, and they'd taken in their niece Rosa Cly as their ward several years ago. During the Season, Rosa circulated among the highest levels of society. But what mattered most to Pearl was that she had some influence with her uncle.

"Oh," the maid said as an afterthought. "You should know, Miss Ivy Bartlett is up there with the mistress."

Pearl thanked her. She knew Ivy from her previous life, as well. Once upon a time, she and Ivy and Rosa had traveled in the same circles. Never exactly friends, but certainly friendly acquaintances.

Pearl hurried through the subterranean corridors of the mansion. She climbed the stuffy, narrow stairwell used by the servants until she reached the floor where Rosa's apartments were located.

There was no one in the wide hallway, and the door to the sitting room stood slightly ajar. Voices drifted out.

"Does she really live there? In the prison."

"Yes, in Marshalsea Prison."

The first voice belonged to Ivy Bartlett; the second was Rosa's.

"How does she tolerate it?"

"She doesn't have much choice, now does she. Besides, she wants to be with her father."

Pearl stopped and put her bag down beside a large Chinese vase outside the door. She wished she could block her ears, but this was surely just an echo of conversations between other members of the *ton* since her father was taken off to debtor's prison.

"How inconsiderate of Perceval Smith not to think of his daughter's future," Ivy said.

"It was certainly irresponsible of him. It's no surprise what happens when you borrow more money than you can afford and then fail to pay it back."

Pearl felt heat rising into her face. She forced herself to stand still, restraining herself from barging in and defending him. This was not what happened to her father. There was *nothing* intentional or fraudulent behind their change of fortune.

Not too long ago, her father had been the most successful importer of fabrics into France and England. He'd been ruined last autumn when the British wartime government seized the assets of his company for doing business with the French before the current outbreak of war.

Now he was languishing in debtors' prison, and Pearl hoped Rosa might help get him out of Marshalsea.

"So, what's she doing here?" Ivy pressed. "She's hardly a trained domestic. What do you have her doing?"

"Sewing, so long as it's not too complicated a job. Sometimes I ask her opinion on dresses I'm planning to have made. She always had a good taste."

Pearl *did* have some knowledge about fabrics. Muslins and Batistes and silks. Classic materials with Etruscan and Egyptian decoration and woven or embroidered borders. Mending dresses to feed herself and her father, however, wasn't something she'd ever imagined doing.

"And she ended up working for you how?"

"She asked me for a job, and I gave it to her."

With Napoleon abdicating last month, Pearl hoped that Rosa would convince Lord Castlereagh to get involved. His lordship certainly had the power to help Percival Smith, and the two men had once been friends. But to approach Rosa and simply ask such a huge favor wasn't conceivable. Working in Londonderry House and appealing to her sense of compassion was another matter.

"You have a heart of gold," Ivy continued. "I wouldn't be so generous."

Pearl couldn't take it anymore. The more she listened, the more she was pained by Ivy's attitude. This was the same response she and her father had received from many of their supposed friends.

Taking a breath to compose herself, Pearl knocked and went in.

The two women were lounging on sofas that faced each other in front of a marble fireplace. The room had been redecorated in the past year, reflecting the simpler tastes of fashion that had been sweeping the homes of the *ton*. Persian carpets filled the floors with symmetrical arrangements of colorful garden flowers. Sheer gauze drapes billowed in front of open windows that faced out onto the green expanses of Hyde Park. A tray filled with pastries and cups of tea—Rosa's late breakfast—sat on a low table between them. A footman stood in attendance in the corner.

"There you are," Rosa said in greeting, brushing her blonde tresses back over her shoulder as she turned to face Pearl. "I was afraid you had already gone for the day."

"Not yet."

"How is your father?"

"A little better. Thank you for asking."

Pearl looked from Rosa to Ivy. The other woman's eyes had turned toward the refreshments on the table. No acknowledgment that they'd ever known each other.

"You remember Miss Bartlett, don't you, Pearl?"

"Of course." She nodded politely. "I hope your mother and sisters are doing well."

Ivy's gaze slowly shifted toward her, but nothing was offered in response. The look was appraising, moving from head to toe, studying every flaw in Pearl's dress and shoes before drifting to the window.

"Ivy and I were just speaking about the ball tonight. I have a favor to ask."

An uncomfortable feeling prickled over her skin. Tonight was Lord and Lady Whitwell's Midsummer Night's Dream Masquerade Ball. The most anticipated and extravagant event of the Season. The guest list included everyone of wealth and importance in London.

"A favor?"

Rosa smiled. "I do love your practical sense, Pearl. No, not a favor. I am asking you to do a job for me."

She waited to hear more.

"As you know, my dress is ready. The mask I intend to wear is here, as well." Rosa glanced at her friend. "Ivy, did I tell you I had it modeled after the one the fairy queen Titania is holding as she turns away from Oberon in that painting at the new gallery in Pall Mall?"

"I have to see it."

Pearl knew all of this. Every step of preparation for the ball had been shared with her. She'd even helped Rosa with the fitting, running gold silk cord lacing through seventeen pairs of eyelets earlier this week while the lady's maid looked on.

"You'll be the most beautiful woman at the ball," Pearl said for the sake of saying something.

"Thank you. But I also need to be ready for any unexpected mishap with the dress."

"Nothing should go awry," Pearl assured her.

Ivy broke in, speaking for the first time since Pearl entered the room. "But something *always* goes wrong, doesn't it?"

"She's right," Rosa agreed. "That's why I want you at the Whitwell House tonight during the ball. Just in case I need you."

Pearl felt the blood drain from her face. Although she'd already guessed the 'favor', the request was crushing. Never mind the fact that she'd be locked out of Marshalsea all night. The possibility of being seen by any of her former friends would be too awful.

Since her father's imprisonment, she'd stayed out of the eye of the *ton*, except for approaching Rosa. Ivy's attitude here was stark affirmation of how others would treat her.

"You will do it. You'll come, won't you?" Rosa asked.

"I..." She tried to come up with an excuse.

"No one will see you," Rosa said in a quiet voice, obviously guessing at Pearl's discomfort. "You'll be below stairs, far from the notice of the guests."

Ivy was watching Pearl like a crocodile eyeing its prey, waiting for her answer.

Pearl wanted to refuse, but she couldn't. She couldn't risk denying Rosa and damaging the connection.

"Very well. I'll be there," Pearl replied. "In the sewing rooms."

"Thank you," Rosa replied. "I was saying to Ivy just before you walked in that you wouldn't abandon me in my time of need."

The underlying meaning in the words struck home. She went out, leaving the door slightly open, as she'd found it. While she picked up her things, snatches of the women's conversation again reached her.

"Who would have thought?" Ivy sounded practically triumphant. "Last year, she was the center of attention for all the men. And tonight she'll be—"

"Considering her circumstances," Rosa interrupted, "Pearl will happily stay out of sight. She won't be competing with you for anyone's attention."

"You're right. But enough about her." Ivy's voice turned conspicuously low. "But on the topic of competition. Is it true that a Persian prince will be attending the Whitwell's ball tonight?"

"Yes, but you can just stay away from him. He's already spoken for."

"I heard he just arrived in London. Spoken for by whom?"

"By me."

Pearl hurried down the hallway. She didn't want to hear about any prince or duke or earl or viscount…or any eligible bachelor whatsoever. So much had changed. Her life had been upended dramatically. Her responsibility now lay with supporting and helping her father.

And right now, she needed to get to the prison and get him settled before leaving him alone for the evening.

2

———

Prince Timour stared out the window of the carriage as it rolled through the streets of London. The route from the embassy had taken them along tree-lined streets, past large stone mansions and broad parklands where patches of rising mist caught the fading glow of the evening.

His cousin, Ali Khan, had been talking continuously. He was a good friend—they'd been companions since childhood—and he'd grown into a man who took quite seriously the tasks that were given to him. Right now, a bit too seriously.

"The ambassador never responded to Lady and Lord Whitwell regarding the way you wish to be introduced at the ball tonight, Hazrat-e Ajal."

Timour glanced at Ali, who rarely addressed him so formally. He was using a title that translated into 'Your Excellency.' The prince sensed a note of nervousness in his friend's tone. All day, he'd been trying to impress on Timour the importance of the evening in completing their diplomatic mission.

"Would you prefer Shahzadeh Timour Mirza…or Prince Timour Mirza? Of course, in either case the British guests will assume Mirza is your last name, rather than a proper address for the Qajar king's son. But I believe that will take less time than having them try to repeat all of your proper names and titles."

Timour recalled a day when the two of them had joked that he needed ten servants and a wagon to carry around his titles.

"It doesn't matter how they introduce me."

"The English people are a peculiar sort. They will insist on knowing just how much deference they need to demonstrate."

Ali Khan was a frequent spokesman in diplomatic situations. He had a cheerful demeanor that hid a shrewd mind. Timour couldn't fathom how his friend had avoided viewing the world with cynicism. As for himself, he saw that people always looked to their own interests. Everyone else be damned was the prevalent attitude.

"You decide."

"Perhaps we should have them announce you as Mirza Timour Khan, Lord High Prince of Iran. Or Shahzadeh. Or Persia's Royal—"

"Decide on one and be done with it, Ali. I really don't care."

Unperturbed by Timour's impatience, he thought about it for a moment before continuing. "Then we shall have them introduce you as Prince Timour Mirza of Persia. Simplicity is the best policy with Englishmen."

Timour waved a hand, totally indifferent to the matter. Several months of travel, with diplomatic stops along the way, had left him bored with formal banquets and entertainments. He was ready to set sail for home. But that wasn't going to happen for another month.

He knew this was an important visit, both for his country and for himself. The peace treaty signed between Russia and Iran last year had made the British nervous. Now the English wanted to make a deal of their own with the Persian government. Timour knew the reason was largely geographic. Iran's location made it a physical buffer between Russian armies and British India.

So, negotiations took place, fortunes were paid, deals were made, and here he was, making good on the last piece of the contract. The English wanted a 'family' connection, and Timour had been ordered by the shah to come to London and choose a wife.

That made this trip highly personal.

"Lord and Lady Whitwell's ball tonight is an extravagant affair," Ali said, breaking into his thoughts. "You, of course, are in courtly regalia. But many guests will be wearing costumes."

"They'll probably think I *am* in costume."

Ali grinned. "That's quite possible."

The prince turned his gaze to the street again as they passed a lamplighter on the sidewalk. "Have they given you the name yet?"

"The name?"

"The name of the woman I am to marry?"

"You have the freedom to choose whomever you wish."

"Do I?"

"Of course."

This would be purely a marriage of diplomacy, and Timour knew exactly how these things worked. The British government surely wanted a spy inside the court of the royal family. Someone to report on the Qajar king's every move. That meant they'd already decided on whose hand he'd be offered. His 'choice' would be severely limited.

"The English are not in the habit of giving up control. They'd never plan a treaty without having the key players selected and in place."

Ali pressed a hand to his heart. "I honestly don't know anything more than what I've already told you."

"Ali, my friend, we're in London for only a month. Don't you have the itinerary that lists the receptions I must attend and whose homes I will visit?"

"I have it here." Ali produced a document. "Every day of our stay in England is scheduled."

"Look down that list. With whom shall I be spending the most time."

Ali ran his eye down the list of events before answering. "Lord Castlereagh, the Foreign Secretary."

"Does Lord Castlereagh have a daughter who is of marriageable age?"

"He has a niece and ward. A Miss Rosa Cly. She is being introduced to you tonight."

"I thought so." Timour was rarely wrong.

He dropped his tall beaver-skin hat on the seat beside him. He then took off the heavy gold chain and the jewel encrusted badge of royalty and the ornate belt of pearls and rubies. He started unbuttoning his coat.

Ali stared, dumbfounded. "What are you doing, Timour? We're almost there."

"Give me your coat."

His cousin shrank back. "No, we're not doing this. You remember what happened last time."

A wry smile pulled at the corner of the prince's lips, but he quickly replaced it with a look of sympathy.

A year ago, they'd swapped places on a visit to Istanbul, and Timour had slipped away. Unfortunately for Ali Khan, he'd been recognized as a substitute right away upon his arrival at the palace on the Bosphorus. Red-faced, he'd borne the brunt of the embarrassment while Timour enjoyed a great night roaming the streets and cafes of that magnificent city. Official letters of apology from the Persian court had followed.

"Ali, there is no one here to recognize us. Besides, it's a ball, a masquerade. It's not an official reception."

"You promised your father you would take this seriously. If this goes badly, you won't suffer. But I'll find myself herding goats through the snows of Mount Damavand...if I'm lucky."

"Don't worry. I intend to take this seriously. Changing places will allow me to see and judge Miss Rosa Cly—who is undoubtedly my future wife—from the safety of your perspective."

"They won't be too thrilled when you suddenly turn up as the real Prince Timour, you know."

"It will be fine. Now hurry up and give me your coat."

Ali Khan smiled weakly as he did as he was directed. "Once again, I'm going into the fire for you, cousin. And we both know who will come out of this with his beard singed."

Timour leaned forward and dressed in the other man's attire. "That's the spirit."

"I assume you want my hat, too."

"No. It's too small."

Ali scoffed and a few moments later, the carriage pulled up to the sidewalk in front of the mansion of Lord and Lady Whitwell. An army of footmen held lanterns as costumed and richly dressed guests disembarked from the line of vehicles and went through the open doors of the entrance. Behind a gate, blazing torches lit up a walkway that appeared to lead to gardens on the side and behind the stately home.

"I'll be in shortly," Timour said to Ali before they climbed out.

"What do you mean? You were to walk in with me. Pretend to be me." There was a note of panic in the other man's tone. "Where are you going?"

"I'm going into those gardens and have a smoke. I'll be in before you get through the receiving line."

A look of resignation settled over Ali. "I've always had a fondness for goats, anyway."

Timour set off along the torch lit path through manicured gardens of greenery and flowers. Darkness was settling in quickly, and the sounds of talk and laughter and orchestral music came from the open doors and windows of the house.

He followed the path for a short distance and wandered from one garden enclosure to the next. Finally, he paused beneath a stone archway covered with climbing roses and looked across a wide square of precisely trimmed greensward, glistening with new-formed dew. Fruit trees cast shadows across portions of walkways.

This was exactly what he was hoping for. What he needed. A peaceful, unplanned moment to himself.

For all of his twenty-eight years of life, from his education to his travels to his residences—even deciding his future wife now—Timour's life had been orchestrated by the king and the court. It was no different from the lot of his older brother, who was first in line to wear the crown. Or the six others ahead of him in the line of succession. To tolerate the velvet chains of his existence, Timour learned early on that he needed to get away by himself. That meant running away. Of course, he always went back, but those few stolen hours or days were a necessity for survival.

He listened to the noises drifting down from the house and patted his coat pocket for his cigar. It wasn't there. He was wearing his cousin's coat.

"*Ali, gonahan neyaz daree.*" Ali, you need some vices.

"What was that rubbish ye just said?" a gravelly voice asked from behind him.

So much for a peaceful moment, Timour thought. Glancing over his shoulder, he made out the bulky shape of a man standing in the darkness. "Not *rubbish*. The words were spoken in a different language. Be on your way."

"What did ye say?"

The English. Already, he wasn't impressed. He waved a hand. "Never mind. What I said wasn't directed at you."

"Who the devil d'ye think ye are?"

Timour let out a frustrated breath and finally turned. There wasn't only one, but two men stood in the shadowy path. They were the same size, as tall as Timour. Their clothing matched the grooms that were running around by the entrance of the house.

"I don't want to get you in trouble. I wasn't speaking to you. Be on your way."

"Get *us* in trouble?"

"Be on our way?" the second man asked, his voice as squeaky as a pig in distress. "What d'ye say, Melvin? How 'bout we teach this one a lesson or two in manners."

Before Timour had a chance to respond, the one named Melvin stepped forward, the end of a club in his hand arcing through the evening air toward the prince's head.

3

———

"You're to go upstairs. Hurry."

Pearl glanced around her at the two other women seated in the sewing room, hoping that the order was directed at them.

"*You*." The maid at the door addressed her directly. "I'm talking to *you*."

Her stomach sank. "Upstairs where?"

"The Ladies' Cloakroom."

Pearl knew from attending the ball last year that many ladies dropped off their wraps before going up to the Great Room. This was *not* what she'd expected in agreeing to come here tonight.

"I don't work for Lord and Lady Whitwell," she protested. "I am not a member of the household."

"Tonight, you are. Come along. Now."

"Ask someone else to go. I'm attending to Miss Rosa Cly. She asked me to stay in the sewing room." Pearl tried to keep her voice steady, devoid of the panic she felt creeping in. She had absolutely no desire to go anywhere that she might run into people she knew.

It was bad enough to be down here. Her reputation had preceded her. She'd heard the whispers start in the Servants' Hall as soon as she arrived. Many of them apparently knew who she was…and what had happened to her father.

"Miss Cly said so," the maid said tersely. "Now, come along. I'll show you the way."

Miss Cly said so. Pearl's knees locked. Was this the reason she was here tonight? Had Rosa planned this?

"We don't have all night. Hurry."

Pearl had no choice but to go. Reluctantly, she stood and followed the servant out of the room, clutching at a glimmer of hope that she'd only be needed there for a short time. Perhaps no one would recognize her. The busy Servants' Hall became oddly quiet as the two women passed through. By the time they reached the stairs, the voices behind her were buzzing with chatter about who she was and where she was going.

At the top of the steps, Pearl found herself in the dimly lit cloakroom occupied only by one harried looking servant. The maid who'd come to fetch her went back down.

"Good thing you're here," the servant whispered as she headed out. "I'm wanted upstairs."

Pearl had received no directions as to what to do, but since the event was a masquerade ball, she prayed very few of the guests would be leaving garments here.

That hope dimmed when a pair of middle-aged ladies

entered, chatting with each other. Pearl curtsied and kept her head down, helping them with their wraps. She'd met one of the women on a number of occasions and recognized the other, but neither even glanced at her. She might as well have been a chair or table. The conversation between them never faltered as they walked out.

"That wasn't so bad," she murmured. Perhaps she'd survive tonight, after all.

She could hear laughter and music drifting down from the Great Room. With a sigh, she moved to a bench near the door and sat down. Her mind turned to her father and the secrets she was keeping from him. He had no idea where she was tonight. She'd lied to him for weeks about Londonderry House and working for Rosa. He believed that there were young women who still welcomed her as a friend during her hours away from Marshalsea.

Pearl stared at groups of people on their way up the marble staircase to the Great Room. Perhaps it was time she spoke with Rosa about what she wanted. Ever since Pearl had been going to Londonderry House to work, she'd never once encountered Lord Castlereagh himself. Gaining an audience with him was the simplest favor she could ask of the niece. Then, she could make her plea directly to the Foreign Secretary.

She heard the effervescent voices of young women approaching the cloak room, and she rose to her feet and moved into a shadowy corner.

"One quick stop."

"Here? What for?"

"You'll soon find out."

Without seeing them, Pearl knew who they were. Rosa, Elizabeth Harris, and Ivy Bartlett. Elizabeth's father was the Ambassador to Spain. She and her family had been away since last Season.

Rosa called in. "Is anyone here?"

The three women crowded the doorway. Pearl slid backward on the seat, wishing the shadows would swallow her hole. Why was Rosa doing this? Her adversary stepped into the room, her eyes focusing on the bench. Pearl was discovered, and embarrassment flushed hot in her face.

"Anyone?" Challenge rang in the other woman's tone.

Pearl stood up. "I'm here."

"Oh, good. I'm so glad you came up from the Servants' Hall." Rosa breezed farther into the cloakroom. "I do hope you don't mind that I offered your services to Lady Whitwell. They needed extra help, and I knew you'd be amenable to—"

"Is there something I can help you with, Miss Cly?" She'd been such a fool, thinking she could trust Rosa, never mind count on her support.

"Pearl? Pearl Smith? Is that you?"

Elizabeth joined Rosa. Ivy remained by the door, a gloating look on her face.

"Oh my Lord! It *is* you. What are you doing here? And what is this thing you're wearing? Is this your costume for the ball?"

"Hardly," Rosa cut in. "Pearl is working, if you can believe it. Actually, she works for me."

"As what? A servant?"

"Seamstress. Servant. Whatever I need her to do. And tonight, I loaned her to Lady Whitwell."

Elizabeth was clearly taken by surprise. "I don't understand. What happened? What did you do?"

Pearl said nothing as another arriving guest entered the cloakroom and removed a light silk wrap. There was no easy answer to the questions. Certainly, nothing she could communicate in a sentence or two. All she could do was to take the insults, one blow at the time. Pearl reached for the lady's garment.

"This is the consequence when one steals," Ivy said.

"*Who* steals?" the newcomer asked, looking alarmed.

"Her father," Rosa replied. "Perceval Smith."

"Perceval Smith, did you say?" The older woman clutched her wrap, unwilling to part with it.

"This is his daughter, Pearl Smith," Ivy told her.

"And you admit to *knowing* her?" the lady asked, shocked.

"Indeed, we were once friends," Elizabeth answered uncertainly.

Pearl forced herself to breathe. Tears burned her eyes, but she wouldn't allow them to fall. They were a pack of wolves, attacking from every side.

"But that was before Perceval Smith became a criminal," Ivy chirped. "My father says he'll rot in Marshalsea, and he's lucky that is the extent of his punishment."

"My uncle is Lord Castlereagh, and he says the same thing," Rosa proclaimed. "But don't forget, ladies, we are all encouraged to practice charity. This one is hardly at fault for her fall. The fact that she is—"

"Excuse me." Pearl could take no more of this. Turning quickly, she fled down the cloakroom stairs.

4

———

THE CLUB FLASHED through the gathering darkness, reflecting the light of a garden torch.

In the blink of an eye, Timour's options raced through his brain. If he tried to back away, the forward motion of the assailant would keep him in range of the weapon. The archway limited the prince's movement to either side.

So, he did what he usually did in a fight, he drove forward. He slammed his forehead into the face of his attacker, and the club flew harmlessly over Timour's shoulder, landing with a thud on the greensward behind him.

The assailant staggered backward a step. His eyes widened in surprise and then lost focus as his knees buckled. The brute sagged and then tumbled onto his side.

Timour had no time to consider the man's condition, however, for the other one was already lunging over the fallen body and squeaking out a high-pitched semblance of a roar. His club hand was upraised, but he stumbled slightly as his shoe buckle caught on the gold braid of his companion's coat.

Stepping forward, Timour raised his left arm to fend off the descending club. Dropping his chin, he planted his right heel, turned his hips, and drove his fist deep into the soft section formed by the V beneath the ribs, exactly in the center of the double rows of buttons.

The blow stopped Squeaker in his tracks and lifted him onto his toes. His chin hit Timour's shoulder, and he wobbled back a step. But he was not ready to quit. Even as he fought to draw a wheezing breath, in his other hand appeared a short-bladed knife. He came at the prince with the look of a killer in his eyes.

Timour had no interest in prolonging the altercation, especially now. Blocking the stabbing motion with his forearm, he delivered another blow to Squeaker's midsection before following with a devastating right that hooked sharply, catching the man on the point of the chin. The other's head snapped around, and he crumpled to the ground.

"A lesson in manners." He picked up the dropped knife, glanced at the motionless assailants, and tossed the weapon into a flower bed.

"Bloody fine work, that!" The voice behind him was cheerful, and Timour turned to see a strapping young fellow in a dark coat, pants, and boots striding across the greensward. He pulled off a shapeless wool hat, ran a hand through unruly hair, and jammed the hat back on. "Well done indeed, mate."

Timour gave him room to pass. His blood was still racing,

and he appraised the newcomer as the young man stopped and prodded the inert bodies with his foot. He carried with him the honest scent of horses and leather. A groom, no doubt.

"These two blokes been throwing their weight around here all day. Acting like they own the place."

"I didn't think for a moment that either of them was Lord Whitwell."

The fellow turned in surprise and then snorted out a laugh. "Aye, his lordship's a mere slip of a fellow compared to them."

"I'll take your word for it."

The young man stuck his hand out and they shook.

"Name's Perkins."

The prince considered his choices for a moment. Whose part was he going to play now? This was certainly an unexpected start to the night.

"Timour."

"Ain't heard that name before. You ain't a Frenchie?"

He shook his head. "No. We just arrived on a ship from St. Petersburg."

Perkins whistled. "Russia. That's far."

"Indeed, it is."

"How long you're staying?"

"About a month, I believe." That was enough about him. "And you? Are you a London man?"

"Not hardly. Country lad, born and bred. I'm a groom in the Whitwells' stables at their place down in Kent."

Timour gestured toward the mansion. "And you're here to help with the ball?"

"Aye. They bring some of us in for part of the Season. They have us lads circling the gardens, staying out of sight, and just being around in case of any trouble. Looks like you found some."

Timour glanced at his fallen foes. "The trouble found me."

"Wrong fellow they picked to mess with."

He was a trained soldier, skilled in the martial arts, and he felt good about taking down both of these armed men. The royal advisors insisted that he travel with dozen bodyguards. But he did what he wanted.

"What're you doing out here, anyway? Servants are supposed to stay with the carriages."

Timour played into the misunderstanding. He didn't feel any need to reveal his identity to the groom. "I had no idea there were rules about where to go or not go, so long as I stay away from the guests."

"Oh, for the likes of you and me, there're plenty of rules."

It was no different in Iran, he thought.

"I should be getting back," Timour said, thinking of his cousin Ali and the promise he'd made of joining him.

"They won't be done up there for a while." Perkins jerked a thumb in the direction of terrace and the open windows of the Great Room above them. "Come along with me."

"Where to?"

"Servant's Hall."

"I'm fine here. My...my master is not planning on staying late at the ball."

"Well, you'd best clean up that mess. And that is some fancy coat your people have their servants wear."

Timour glanced down at where the groom gestured. A few drops of blood stained Ali Khan's coat.

"You're bleeding from above your peeper."

Timour pulled off a glove and raised a hand to his eyebrow. He had indeed opened a cut there.

"It is nothing."

"Maybe to you," Perkins said. "But I know the butler here would shit a firestorm if one of us had blood on *our* coat. Come on. We'll get you fixed right up."

Timour thought about it. He could go to the ball before getting cleaned up and draw all kinds of unwanted attention. Or he could keep walking about out here. He now had a good excuse not to show his face upstairs. There were plenty of more opportunities this month for these Englishmen to lure him toward the wife they intended to entrap him with.

First things first.

"You say there is a place where I can put myself back in order?"

"Aye, there's a washroom by the housekeeper's rooms. I'll show you the way. And you know, since you're new to town, this'd be a cracking time to meet some of the folks you'll be seeing around."

Timour doubted he would again be walking off the way he did tonight.

"With the ball and all, most every household has a servant

or two down below stairs here. And it'll get lively, too. I know a footman from Lord Castlereagh's brought his fiddle. The lasses will be kicking their heels up, to be sure."

"That does sound more interesting than the event above."

"Aye, mate, by a Scotch mile."

Timour nodded at the fallen footmen. They were starting to stir. "What about them?"

The groom scoffed and spit on the ground near them. "Don't you worry none about them boneheads. They'll find their way back to where they belong. Nobody in the Whitwell household is going to be too worried about 'em, I can tell you that."

As Timour walked beside his chatty new friend, he recalled how nervous Ali Khan was about this deal with the English, especially tonight. His decision was made. He'd go back upstairs after he cleaned the blood from his face and coat.

It took only a few minutes to make their way out of the gardens and around the house to a walled-in yard. A number of men and women were busily carrying things in and out. They all exchanged cheerful greetings and looked with interest at Timour.

Perkins led him inside. They skirted the kitchens and stopped by a closed door.

"You can get cleaned up in here, mate. I'll be back."

"Thank you."

"No worries." Perkins saluted and started back down the corridor. "Wait till the lads hear how you handled them gorillas."

As the groom disappeared around the corner, Timour opened the door and went in. The room had a large tub in the center of the floor. Pitchers and washbasins sat on a long counter on the far wall beneath three windows. A young woman was standing by one of them.

Timour cleared his voice and she turned quickly, facing him. He saw the tears glistening on her face.

5

"My sincere apologies for intruding, miss."

Pearl quickly wiped the tears of anger and embarrassment from her face. "Not at all. I...I was just leaving."

When she'd escaped the cloakroom, all she wanted was to find somewhere private to hide and collect herself. The women upstairs, her ex-friends, behaved as if they had a vendetta. Pearl didn't know what she'd done or how she'd insulted them to warrant that kind of ruthless treatment in return. Still, running away, she had to remind herself how much there was at stake. And she couldn't lose hope, based on what she'd heard about Lord Castlereagh's feelings toward her father. That was merely an offhand comment.

The downstairs Servants' Hall was brimming with activity. The washroom had seemed the logical place to escape to.

A single candle burned in a sconce on the wall. More light poured in from the hallway. The stranger standing in the open doorway was tall, but his face was in shadow.

"There is no need for you to go. I shall wait outside."

There was no one working in the cloakroom but her. Pearl imagined she was in a great deal of trouble with Rosa. Still, she needed to go back. She couldn't afford to burn the bridge entirely. If it wasn't already too late.

"Please. I insist. I'm finished here."

Pearl had traveled with her father since she was waist high, and she had a rudimentary knowledge of a few languages. This man had an accent she couldn't exactly place. The dark coat he wore was decorated with gold braid across his broad chest. The buttons were covered in fine gold cloth. The quality of the tailoring and the costliness of the fabric were far superior to any other servant she'd seen tonight.

Her curiosity about the stranger hardly mattered at the moment. No doubt, trouble was waiting for her upstairs. She had to apologize and hide her embarrassment. She let out a frustrated breath and wiped the escaping string of tears. And she wondered how many more guests Rosa was planning to usher in and out of the cloak room tonight. She started for the door.

"You've read the ending."

His deep voice stopped her. Now, only a step away, she could see his face. His short hair was dark, almost black in this light, as was his full beard. He was young and extremely handsome, with high, chiseled cheekbones and a straight nose. He had a cut and bruise on his eyebrow, and the blood on his face and coat explained his appearance in the washroom.

"The ending?" she asked.

"You're not the only one. It makes everyone cry."

"What does?"

"The story of Rustam and Sohrab, of course. In the *Shah-nameh*, the Book of Kings."

Pearl was fond of books, and she had a good memory for what she'd read. "I wish I had read it, but I haven't. Is it new?"

"Fairly new. Ferdowsi wrote it only eight hundred years ago." There was a twinkle of humor in his eyes.

"Oh, quite recent. I shall look for it the next time I am in a bookshop."

"I wish it were that easy. I would assume you do not read Farsi."

He waited for her to answer, and she shook her head.

"So, your only chance of reading this collection of epic poems would be to find a translation," he explained. "And the only translation into English that I know of is being done by a Mathew Lumsden in British India. He has eight volumes planned, but so far, he has only managed to publish the first. And just today, sadly, I was informed that no bookshop in London can supply a copy."

Pearl tried to untangle the man's speech. Above stairs or below, she'd never heard anyone speak so articulately about a work of literature to a stranger.

"Farsi!" she exclaimed. "I just made the connection. Do you mean Persian?"

"Native speakers prefer the term Farsi."

Bits of the conversation she'd heard this morning as she left Londonderry House came back to her. "You are...you are..."

The man's uninjured eyebrow shot up.

"You must be one of the Persian prince's companions."

"Companion?" He paused and then shook his head. "Merely a lowly servant."

"Not *merely* a servant, I think. You must also be a tutor to his highness."

"I shall be sure to suggest to the prince that he grant me a new title." He bowed to her. "Now, I shall wait outside until you have vacated the room, Miss...Miss..."

She dropped a small curtsy. "Pearl Smith."

"And I am..." He stopped as the sound of a man's voice from down the hallway reached them.

"Timour, are you done sprucing yourself up, mate? The folk in the Hall are eager to meet you."

"Indeed," he called out. "Almost ready."

He began to back out the door.

"Please wait." She went quickly to one of the wash basins, soaked a clean cloth, and brought it back, offering it to him. "The spots on your coat shall only spread if you try to clean them right now. But you can use this to wipe the blood on your brow."

Their fingers brushed as he accepted the cloth from her hand.

"How did this happen?"

"The minor risk of a foreigner walking in an English garden." He dabbed at his face but missed most of it.

She didn't know what he meant but didn't pursue him for a clearer answer. "Would you allow me?" She motioned to his brow.

"I should be much obliged."

Pearl took the cloth back, but an awkward moment pursued. He was quite tall, and she didn't want to step too close. Finally, he tipped his head so she could reach.

His skin was warm. She tried to stare only at the place where the blood had dried by his temple. But she could feel the weight of his gaze on her face, and her cheeks caught fire. Her body warmed. A delicious twist moved low in her stomach.

Pearl bit her lip, thinking how this situation—the two of them alone in this room—could ruin her reputation forever. What was left of it.

Sadness came like a blast of cold air, slapping her awake. She wasn't the person she'd once been. She never would be again. Pearl hurriedly removed the last of the blood on his face and stepped back. "That's better. You're fit to return to public."

He straightened up but didn't move. "You are sad again. And I cannot blame Ferdowsi for it. Why? What's wrong?"

She shook her head, embarrassed at being so transparent.

"Come along, Timour." The same voice as before called from the hall. "People are waiting."

"Can I be of any help to you?" The gallant man wasn't to be hurried. "Anything you need. Ask and it shall be done."

"I'm fine. In fact, I'm needed upstairs. Please go."

His eyes met hers and she was taken aback by the depth of sympathy she saw there. More raw emotions welled up in her. For months now, Pearl and her father had been alone. No one cared. They had no friends left. No one deigned to hear their pleas. And here she was standing before a total stranger...and *he* cared.

"Miss Pearl Smith, I must tell you, meeting you here has been both a surprise and a delight." He bowed once more. "I wish you a pleasant and happier evening."

He backed out of the room and disappeared down the hallway as Pearl wiped away a newly shed tear.

6

———

Upon first entering the washroom, Timour had seen a woman of medium height with brown hair and a pleasantly shaped face. She was too thin for what he generally found attractive. But after only a few moments in Pearl's company and a closer look, his assessment sharpened.

Her hair was a glossy chestnut color, shot with wisps of copper that danced in the flickering light. Her mouth was wide, her lips full, her cheeks pink. Her eyes were large and shone like jeweled amber. She had the grace and loveliness of the women portrayed in Persian miniature paintings. A moon-faced woman, as the classical poets wrote.

She was beautiful and interesting, but her sadness distressed him. She tried to hide it, but the melancholy emanated from her very soul. He wanted to do something, help her.

He looked back at the door to the washroom, wondering if she was coming out, as well. She wasn't.

Perkins was standing at the end of the corridor, exchanging quips and looks with maids and serving women who were passing. He grinned and slapped Timour on the shoulder. "Finally. There's a sorry lot of lads in the Hall looking to raise a glass to you."

"Has anyone seen to those men outside?"

"They're fine, mate. Off licking their wounds. We're celebrating. That's all you need to know."

The friendly cheer of a dozen men and women went up as they entered the Servants' Hall. Some of the men were dressed in livery, others clothed more like Perkins. From their apparel, they appeared to come from a number of different households. They openly gawked at Timour, studying him from head to toe.

He wore a long coat of dark gray silk, adorned with braid, loose pants, and beaded slippers. None of the men wore beards, as he did. He'd already noticed that the custom was not fashionable in London, as it was elsewhere.

"And this here is the man of the hour." Perkins took his arm and pulled him forward. "A Russky, fresh off the boat and straight into Melvin's nightmares."

This attention was not what he was looking for. "Not Russia. I am from Iran...Persia."

"What's the difference?" Perkins joked. "Russian or Persian. Gog or Magog. It's all the same to us, mate. Ain't it, lads?"

"Long as we can drink to it," someone replied, drawing a guffaw from the others.

Gog? Magog? Timour had no idea what Perkins was referring to. But regarding the difference in countries, this wasn't the place for a lecture in geography.

Someone shoved a glass into his hand as the servants gathered around him. From the comments being directed at him, it sounded like everyone was glad the two footmen outside got what was coming to them.

"That Melvin's got no more wit than a stewed prune."

"Aye, I'm glad he's got a good thrashing, puke stocking rascal that he is."

"And that rooting hog Jack ain't no better."

"He's quick enough to point that toad-sticker at ye."

"Them two loons is nothing without t'other. A pair of rank, cream-faced rascals, the two of 'em."

"And this Russky Beau Brummel thumped 'em both."

"Aye, that he did." Perkins raised his cup. "To Timothy... and the sweet sound of cracked heads."

"Timour," the prince corrected, but no one paid the least attention.

As the rest of the gathering emptied their cups, Timour raised his glass to his nose. Smelling liquor, he lowered it. The servants smacked their lips, and the glasses and cups were quickly presented for a refill.

"Make it another, mate. A good thrashing is worth a drop or two."

"Especially for them fools. Melvin and Jack ain't got three inches between 'em, the buggering whoresons. Pour it out, lad."

There were a few men in the Qajar court who drank wine in private. But there were many more who followed the *deen,* abstaining from alcohol. Though he didn't judge those who imbibed, Timour was not one of them. He didn't intend to drink now.

"This is fine brandy," someone exclaimed. "Ye can taste the peaches in it."

"Aye, we got four bottles that ain't making it into the punch upstairs."

"Lovely. Pour it afore it goes bad."

As they laughed, Timour had a good idea that the drinking had begun some time before he gave them reason.

"Pour another for Timothy."

The prince shook his head and glanced at the nearly empty bottle. "I must be leaving you."

"He ain't even touched it," the bottle bearer announced.

Someone else approached and took a look. "Ain't our nantz good enough for ye?"

The question didn't deserve an answer.

"Ye got better in Russky land?"

"Maybe it's the company."

"Maybe we ain't hoity-toity enough for a foreign dandy to be drinking with."

Everyone was talking at once, and Timour felt the sense of fellowship slip away. He cared nothing for what these people said. His silence and the brooding look he sent their way finally got their attention. They gradually grew quiet, waiting for his response. The eyes boring into him were as cool as a winter wind off Mount Damavand.

The liveried footman holding the bottle prodded him with it. "Drink, man."

The prince shook his head. "Thank you. No."

"I ain't asking, mate. Drink."

"I do not drink alcohol." He tried to keep his voice steady, not let his temper get away from him.

A serving woman chirped accusingly. "I worked with Russky servants afore. They drink like fish. I seen 'em."

"I am not Russian." Timour turned to the groom. "The ship I was traveling on made port in Russia before sailing here."

"What are ye, a Turk?" another man asked.

"He don't drink. It's clear as glass. He's a bloody Saracen, he is."

The crowd around him visibly shrank back from Timour, and the expressions were uniformly hostile.

"I've heard warnings about your lot," a young woman murmured. "You're here to steal white women for them sultans."

Timour's stare was sharp enough that she backed away, edging behind a groom. He was not about to engage in this foolishness, but the irony did not escape him. He was only here because the damned English were foisting one of *their* women off on him.

"Aye. A lass was took from Limehouse not a fortnight ago. Stole by a bloody dinge. This could be the very fella."

Timour felt the spikes of anger heating in his brain. These people were ignorant fools. It had been a mistake to come in here. Thinking that someone who looked and dressed differently would not be harassed by the English was foolish too. Ali Khan had been right. Now, he would very likely need to fight his way past these people, through the kitchens, and out the door.

"He's a bloody Moor!"

"Confess!" A young fellow slammed his cup on the table. "You're a Barbary pirate!"

"That it, mate?" Perkins asked, accusation painted across his features. "You a Mohammedan? You worship the horned devil himself?"

Timour had no interest in explaining that his brethren worshiped one God and not the prophet, if that's what the man meant. "I am Muslim."

"Ye killed Jesus!" another woman cried out.

They didn't even know their own faith. Timour shook his head, doing his best to restrain his anger. The depth of the ignorance in those surrounding him was apparently without measure. He looked for a place to put the glass down. "I am leaving."

"No, mate." Perkins stepped in front of him. "You ain't going nowheres till you drink with us."

"And tell us the truth about what you're doing here," the bottle-bearer growled.

He was indeed going to be fighting his way out.

"Back away from him! All of you." A woman's angry voice rang out from behind Timour. "Back away this moment, you fools."

The words were sharp, and everyone turned to look for the speaker.

"Have you gone mad? *This* is how you treat a guest?"

Timour turned around. Miss Pearl Smith had her hands on her hips. Her face was crimson and her eyes blazing.

"For shame!" she continued hotly. "The man does not drink alcohol. He is simply practicing his religion. Rather than acting like an unruly mob—devoid of virtue and hospitality—perhaps you should subdue your...your *irrational* pride and give thanks instead for the *undeserved* mercy which the Lord has bestowed upon you!"

7

PEARL SHOULD HAVE GONE BACK UPSTAIRS, but her curiosity about the man delayed her. Instead of returning directly to the Ladies' Cloakroom, she'd followed Timour and the groom down to the Servants' Hall. And as she listened to the conversation from the side, a sick feeling settled in her gut.

She'd held her tongue for as long as she could, but every eye was on her now.

"For shame!" she said again.

Shocked silence pervaded the room. Timour pushed his glass into Perkins hand, and the groom took it from him.

She needed to go. She wasn't concerned with the hard looks, and Timour was perfectly capable of taking care of himself. In the face of the insults, he'd remained composed, even aloof. She sensed that tonight wasn't the first time he'd run into such ignorance.

Timour started toward her, brushing the servants aside. As the murmurs began, she decided to wait for him. The whispers were all around them. Everyone was talking at the same time.

"How do they know each other?"

"He thinks he's better than us, he does."

"Who is the bloke, really?"

"Did you see the way he looked at us?"

"There's a prince upstairs, I heard."

"Acts like royalty. Maybe he goes with the prince."

Timour's dark eyes never left Pearl's face as he moved through the throng. Upon reaching her, he offered her his arm as if they were processing in to dinner.

"Miss Smith, would you care to accompany me?"

She placed her hand on his solid forearm, having no idea where he was leading her. One thing she was sure of, she had no interest in staying in this room another moment. Or in this house, if she could help it.

Having witnessed the verbal abuse Timour had endured from these servants, she thought of the people they worked for. Then, the events that occurred upstairs reasserted themselves in her mind, and she recognized the truth. Rosa's cruelty had been intentional, and that forced Pearl to accept the fact that she'd been building her hopes on treacherous sands.

Before they could reach the door, a sharp voice rang out from the passageway to the kitchens.

"Begone from here, ye rascals. Every one of ye." The second cook, a pinch-faced, youngish man with a bald shiny pate and a northern accent, stood glaring at the servants, butcher knife in hand. "If ye got naught to do, I've got plenty o' work for all of ye."

The crowd scattered like mice, scurrying off in every direction. In a moment, the hall was empty, leaving only Pearl and Timour. The cook eyed them suspiciously, but then nodded and stalked off back to the kitchens.

"Thank you for coming to my rescue, Miss Smith."

"You hardly needed anyone's help. I only spoke to ease my own anger."

He led her out into the walled-in service yard. Some of the servants who'd been in the hall were now standing in groups, whispering to others who, in turn, openly gaped at them.

Without paying any attention to them, Timour took her through a gate and into the formal gardens.

"How could you remain so calm, surrounded by such scurrilous behavior?"

"Calm?" he scoffed. "A person in my position becomes quite practiced in the art of pretending."

Pretending! Pearl thought of her own life and the fate of her father. Except for falling apart in the cloakroom tonight, she'd become exceptionally good at pretending too.

Lamps lit the paths, and the moon was high in the May night sky. She turned her eyes to the terrace and the open windows and doors of the Great Room, where she could hear laughter and waltz music in the air.

They paused in the path, and she removed her hand from his arm. Against the garden wall behind a bench, pear trees had been carefully trained along trellises above a bed of flowers. The voices of grooms and drivers and the sounds of horses came from beyond the wall. The scent of roses hung in the air.

"Tell me, why *did* you speak up on my behalf, Miss Smith?"

"There is a saying that *ignorance leads to fear, fear leads to hatred, and hatred leads to violence.*"

"Indeed. The words of Abū al-Walīd Muḥammad ibn Aḥmad ibn Muḥammad ibn Rushd."

"Who?"

"The philosopher Ibn Rushd. The English publish him under the name Averroes. Have you read his work?"

He continued to surprise her. "I have. But I couldn't have told you his full name for a thousand pounds."

Timour shrugged. "Where I come from, a person's name conveys nearly everything one needs to know about them. A name is valued."

"In England, a person's name is valued, as well."

"As long as it is not too long or too difficult to pronounce."

"Touché."

He inclined his head slightly. "But I should not tease you when you have had a difficult day."

"I'm feeling better out here in the fresh air. But now you've piqued my interest. So, what is *your* full name?"

"Mine?" He paused as a shout came from the men beyond the wall, followed by gruff laughter.

"Yes, yours."

"My name is Timour Mirza." He bowed. "And now you know everything there is to know about me."

"I doubt it." The urge to smile immediately gave way to

seriousness. "I should like to apologize on behalf of my countrymen. There is no excuse for the way they spoke to you in there."

"If they are like the servants in my country, they are men and women who have seen little of the world. And *you* have nothing to apologize for. Still, I wonder how civil their masters would be upstairs."

Exactly what she'd been thinking.

"Oh, I believe you'd find them to be civil enough. If one dresses well or, better yet, if one has a title to throw at them, the *ton* tend to be all smiles." Pearl looked up at the open windows. "But the masks they're wearing tonight make it easier to hide their malice. And believe me, they are far more practiced than their servants when it comes to striking when you least expect it."

"It sounds as if you have suffered from their venom?"

"A lowly seamstress? No one in that ballroom would condescend to even think of me."

Except Rosa and Ivy. She'd indeed felt their fangs. There was no doubt in her mind what they intended by exposing her in that cloakroom.

He paused a moment. "Do you need to go back?"

Pearl was undecided, unable to completely surrender the fading hope that Rosa might help her. If she didn't go back, that avenue would surely be closed to her. Then there was now. Standing in a garden with a handsome, intelligent stranger, carrying on an enjoyable conversation.

While she was contemplating an answer, a footman holding a lamp came hurrying along the path. He stopped when he spotted them. "Oi, there! You're Pearl Smith, ain't ye?"

The young man's tone was sharp, and Pearl looked over at him, feeling her anger flare. "Do I know you? Can I help you?"

"Your mistress, Miss Cly, wants ye upstairs in the Ladies' Cloakroom now. She don't pay you to be dallying below stairs, says she. And I don't need to be chasing after ye out here. Now, come along and make it quick."

Pearl felt the heat building behind her eyes. Rosa wasn't done. She was intent on embarrassing her, again and again.

"Enough of that," Timour commanded sharply. "You will return to the house. Tell Miss Cly that Miss Smith was called away on an emergency."

The young man stared at him for a long moment, and Pearl thought trouble was about to break out.

But then the footman shrugged. "She won't be happy, mate."

"I am not your mate. Go and do as you've been told. *Now!*"

"Aye, sir." The footman turned on his heel and trotted off.

Pearl looked up at Timour, feeling a little lost for words. He stood calmly in the shadows, but his tone conveyed the authority of one who was accustomed to giving orders. Since her father's arrest and detention at the Marshalsea debtors' prison, no one had spoken on her behalf. No one had honestly acted as a friend or shown any kind of protectiveness.

"Is there a place where a first-time traveler to London might find a meal at this time of night, Miss Smith?"

Pearl took a moment to gather her emotions and find her voice. "At the house?"

"No. I will not be returning there. Somewhere, perhaps, away from here."

Places where she'd dined in her previous life were expensive. There were, however, a number of chop houses along Piccadilly, and she knew of a coffee house in Covent Garden where the meals were acceptable.

"Perhaps you could try the Rainbow Coffee House in Covent Garden. It is quite respectable. But it is some distance from here."

"Close enough to walk on a mild, moonlit May evening?"

"I should think so."

"Very well. Then would you be kind enough to serve as guide and dine with me as my guest?"

The invitation was unexpected. If she dined with him, their time together wouldn't be finished. She'd heard the expression, *ships passing in the night*. If she turned down his offer, they would walk away and never see each other again.

"I assure you that my intentions are completely honorable." Timour placed a hand over his heart. "You will be in no danger. We shall have dinner, engage in some conversation—on philosophy, perhaps—and walk back here afterward."

Pearl didn't know him, but she felt perfectly at ease with him. He was handsome, intriguing, and worldly. And in the end, what did she have to lose by accompanying him?

Nothing. She couldn't go back to Marshalsea until morning, anyway.

"I'd be honored to dine with you."

8

THE NEW SIDEWALKS along Piccadilly were filled with people walking and enjoying the mild night. The young woman walked beside Timour, and they spoke only occasionally.

The street itself was generally crowded with carriages and with vendors hawking their wares. In an odd way, the liveliness of the place reminded him of the streets of Isfahan and the grand bazaar. On a night like this, the shops and tables of craftsmen and food sellers in the stone-vaulted lanes surrounding Naqsh-e Jahan Square would be filled with the people of the city.

Timour waved off a young man offering to sell them a sheet of paper containing the ballad of a recently executed highwayman of some notoriety.

London was an interesting city. He wondered, though— thinking of the woman walking beside him—if he would have said so an hour ago.

The initial perceptions of a place—or a person—were

difficult to change. Timour found that the judgment he made about someone on their first meeting was generally sound. The entire future of his relationship was often based on those impressions.

Pearl Smith. Her beauty aside, the young woman's manner, intelligence, outspokenness, and courage had left him with the most favorable impression. So much so that he wanted to spend time with her. He wanted to get to know her better.

In contrast, there was Rosa Cly, whom he was intended to meet this evening. He hadn't met Lord Castlereagh's niece, but he was already forming a judgment about her from the message she'd sent with the footman. It was one thing to send for someone. It was quite another to encourage insolence in the messenger. Rosa Cly's words had done exactly that.

The prince could already hear the argument Ali Khan would present. *Timour, you don't know what exactly was said....The footman could have elaborated on the original order. Blame it on the style of the delivery of the messenger....You have a responsibility to your father.*

From experience, the prince knew that people rarely revealed their true selves in diplomatic situations. Himself included. But Rosa Cly hadn't expected him to witness the delivery of her message.

He was here in England with a royal directive to choose and marry a stranger and bring her back to his home. The intention...to seal a treaty with a marital contract. Still, Timour's preference would be to bring back someone who would look upon her adopted people with some semblance of decency and respect.

He was glad he'd eluded any introduction to Miss Cly this evening. Eventually, he would meet her—tomorrow or one of the days following. He was certain Lord Castlereagh would throw them together quite soon, unless he did something about it.

He glanced at the profile of his companion. Pearl Smith appeared to be lost in thought.

"The woman who sent the footman after you." He waited until her face turned to his. "Is she a cruel person?"

"I wouldn't say that."

"But when I found you in the washroom. You were upset. Was she not responsible for it?"

"She is not responsible for my situation."

"That is an evasion. Are you trying to protect her?"

"Why should I?"

"I don't know. Perhaps because you are both women, because you are both English, and I am a foreigner."

"I have a life that has nothing to do with Miss Cly. Sadness can be caused by misfortune, by an unlucky twist of fate."

She stopped talking as two street urchins, no more than nine or ten years old, raced across the street toward them. As the red-faced boys weaved between a carriage and a sedan chair, they drew the shouts of a driver and a footman, but they didn't slow down. The two came within a yard of Timour and Pearl before darting up a dark alley. One of them was carrying a live chicken under his ragged jacket.

So, England had its petty thieves, as well.

"But you were saying something about an unlucky twist of fate, Miss Smith. What misfortune has befallen you, if I might ask?"

"And here we are at Leicester Square."

It was obvious she was deliberately ignoring his question.

She gestured to a city square, surrounded by a wrought iron fence and filled with rows of trees and walkways. A statue of a gentleman on a horse gleamed in the moonlight. "That is a statue of King George the First. It was recently re-gilt, I believe."

"He is indeed a striking figure, but I believe you're trying to distract me."

"You're correct."

"But why? I mean no harm. I'm only curious—"

"Is this why you asked me to accompany you for dinner, sir?" she interrupted. "To question me about my employer?"

"No. Of course not."

Timour recognized his error. Rosa Cly was nothing to him. He needed no excuses to reject her as a potential wife. The wrong color of her slippers would be enough. At the same time, he was here, free for an evening in London, walking beside a beautiful and intriguing woman. One he wished to learn more about.

"My curiosity has caused me to forget my manners. My sincerest apologies." He meant every word. She wasn't one of his subjects.

Her pretty face lifted, and she stared into his eyes for few heartbeats. "I believe you."

He held her gaze. "Thank you. Now, let's talk about you."

"About me?"

"Who are you really?"

"I told you. My name is Pearl Smith."

"Beyond that. Those servants deferred to you when you spoke to them."

"I'd like to think they were embarrassed by their actions."

"No, I think not. I perceive a great divide between you and them, Miss Smith. You're well-read, educated."

"What makes you think that?"

"For one thing, you can quote a philosopher such as Averroes."

"You mean Abū al-Walīd Muḥammad...Ibn Rushd." She paused. "But I still can't remember the rest of his name."

"You remembered that after hearing it only once?"

"I am fond of learning."

"It's more than that. You're well educated."

"You might be making too many assumptions."

He shook his head. "On certain matters, I'm never wrong."

Timour knew his questioning was intrusive, bordering on impertinent. He guessed he was nothing like the English men Pearl spent time with. Still, she walked beside him, seemingly unoffended by his probing. "Now, let me see. I shall need to examine your knowledge of history, geography, and rhetoric."

She laughed. She obviously knew that he was joking.

"You have already proven that you are well-versed in languages."

"When on earth did I do that?"

"When I referred to Farsi. Persian. You didn't think that meant I was Russian or Prussian or Arab or Indian."

She scoffed. "You're giving me far too much credit as to what I know and what I don't know."

"*Vous êtes éduqué, admettez-le.*"

"I might simply pretend I didn't understand what you just said."

"I see the smile on your face. So it's already too late. Which also tells me you are not an actress." Timour brushed the back of his hand against hers. "Let me add that to what I know. Aside from having read Averroes, you speak French."

"You are quite the inquisitor, sir."

"Indeed. When I have a subject that interests me."

Pearl's face took on a pink shade, and she looked away.

Timour discreetly kept an eye on her as they strolled along. There was a loveliness about her that was as unassuming as it was captivating. She spoke proudly of this part of London; she sounded as if she had been raised in this very neighborhood. She pointed out several houses facing the square that she said belonged to people of literary and political note. Something about her tone made him suspect she had been a guest in them.

"This is all very interesting, Miss Smith, but I'd like to know more about you. In fact, I want to know *everything* about you."

She stopped and faced him at the far corner of the square. A narrower lane lay ahead, filled with more pedestrians than carriages. Lamps hung at intervals from the walls of shops and houses.

"I thought we were going to have a simple conversation and dine together."

"Are we not having a simple conversation?"

She slowly shook her head, studying his face. "Perhaps we can proceed differently. We can both act as inquisitors. How would you feel about answering a question of mine for every one that you ask? We can get to know each *other*."

Timour had no interest in talking about himself. Once people found out who he was, they never treated him the same.

He smiled and waved his hand at their surroundings. "You were telling me about the neighborhood. Are we still near the royal palace?"

"Much better. Indeed, we are not far from St. James's Palace, though I don't think they are expecting us to call on them this evening." They started walking again with Pearl explaining how the King's Mews was located only a few streets down toward the river. "The buildings house the Guards and the royal stables. Some exceptionally fine horses, I'm told."

"Never visited it?" he asked.

She hid a smile. "No, but I've often passed by it. Quite impressive."

Just then church bells all around them began to toll the hour.

"I have heard of St. Martins-in-the-Fields Church. Are some of the bells we're hearing coming from there?"

"It's just there." Pearl pointed down a busy lane they were crossing. "That, I *have* visited."

The idea of this young woman working in the Whitwell's cloakroom was simply too farfetched to be believed. She'd spoken earlier of a twist of fate. Fortunes changed and there were many causes for it. War. Bad investments. The loss of a parent. Illness. He'd met many people in his life who'd suffered reverses of fortune. But that was where the aid and comfort of old friends came in.

But perhaps she had none.

"Here we are. Covent Garden."

The open square was surprisingly large and filled with people, despite the late hour. This was one of the places that he'd heard the wealthier classes of London came to play.

Along one side of the long rectangular space, a row of arches created a piazza, not unlike some he'd seen in Florence and other Italian cities. The center held a market area with a low white fence all around it. Shops lining the inside of the fence were doing a brisk business, as were the dozens of eating and drinking establishments in the buildings facing the square.

"Is that the Theatre Royal there in the corner of the market?"

"Yes, it is."

The building boasted a fine structure of a classical design. A line of torches lit the sidewalk in front of the place.

"A friend of mine recommended this as the very place I should visit when I came to London."

"Your friend is English?"

"Indeed."

"What is his name?"

"You don't know everyone who resides in London, do you?"

"We live in a smaller world than you imagine. People know each other, and if not, they talk about the other."

"Byron." The man was a fascinating character—albeit a heavy drinker—and brilliant with a flair for anything shocking or flamboyant. His stories about the gambling "hells" and the brothels around Covent Garden were as colorful as they were entertaining.

"You *know* Lord Byron?" For the first time, Pearl looked impressed.

"Only casually. We've had some interesting conversations."

"Where did you meet him?"

"Portugal."

Byron had told him he'd read about the Ottoman and Persian lands as a child. He was attracted to Islam—especially to Sufi mysticism—and the two of them had spent many an enjoyable day sailing or dining together and discussing the culture of Timour's homeland.

"When was this?"

"Five years ago, I believe. In Lisbon."

"Mr. Mirza, I think you have not been forthright with me." Her brows drew together. "You are *not* a servant. *Not* a tutor. You are *not* at all who you say you are."

9

———

"I BELIEVE neither of us are *exactly* what we say we are. Is that not true, Miss Smith?"

Pearl paused as two gentlemen strolled by them. One of them nodded to her as the other continued to speak loudly about the abysmal state of literature currently being published.

There was no point in denying her companion's assertion. He was right. He knew her name, but she had indeed been less than forthright about herself. He had no idea about her background, her father, or the circumstances that had put him in prison.

Actually, it felt good to be able to walk beside someone and not feel the need to explain. No need to worry about what falsehoods he might have heard.

"I have been truthful about my name," she countered.

"As have I. But perhaps I spoke in error earlier when I said a name provided everything important about a person."

"What's in a name? A rose—"

"By any other name would smell as sweet," he finished.

"You even know *Romeo and Juliet*?"

"My teacher told me that Shakespeare is a poet for all the world." Wrinkles of amusement creased the corners of his dark eyes. "Besides, tragedy suits the Persian temperament."

A child approached them, holding bouquets of flowers. "Forget me nots?"

Pearl began to shake her head when her companion handed her a coin. The flower-girl's eyes opened wide. "Ye want 'em all?"

"One lovely bouquet will do," he said.

Taking the delicate cluster of blue flowers, he presented them to Pearl. She was grateful and surprised.

"Why...thank you."

He gestured to a sign hanging depicting a rainbow over a nearby doorway. "And is this where we are to dine?"

She nodded and started toward the door. "Do you realize you gave her enough money to feed her for a fortnight."

"I am glad I was able to do it."

Generosity was a lost quality amongst people she'd once known.

The smell of coffee and roasting beef greeted them as they entered the Rainbow, along with the stares of the dozen or so men and women scattered at tables around the place. Conversations ceased. On the right wall, a small fire was burning in a large fireplace, adding unnecessary warmth but lending a coziness to the atmosphere. A woman in a mobcap and an apron was standing behind a counter, directing several waiters with a long wooden spoon like a conductor at the opera.

One of the men, wearing a short brown jacket over a worn black vest approached them, wiping his hands on an apron that draped from his waist. His hair was curled in the latest fashion but stuck straight up in several places. His eyes had the harried look of a hunted rabbit.

Timour Mirza addressed him, and every eye in the place turned in their direction. Her companion, tall and almost regal, had the bearing of a man who was accustomed to being served.

"Aye, sir. Aye. Will that table along the wall suit ye?" The waiter gestured toward a table in front of a bench.

Receiving a nod, he hurried ahead of them. With a cloth he produced from somewhere, he swept crumbs from the white tablecloth onto the floor. They sat side-by-side, facing the room, and Pearl placed her flowers on the table.

The server recited the short list of items available.

"Miss Smith, would you be kind enough to order for both of us?"

She recalled his objection to drinking alcohol back in Whitwell House. Pearl wished she knew more about what Muslims could eat. "As you can tell, the selection of food is limited. Do you have a preference of what I should order?"

"I am a traveler in your country. You are my sole person of trust. Whatever you choose will be excellent."

She appreciated his faith in her. "Do you have any objection to fish?"

"None whatsoever."

As the server hurried off, Pearl turned toward the handsome man seated beside her. His attention was on the room and the other patrons, and this allowed her to study his features. He had a certain quality about him that one saw in classical paintings. But whatever she thought of his looks, it was the confidence he exuded that impressed her even more.

After losing her mother at a young age, Pearl had been raised by her father. As she grew to adulthood, she'd always preferred his company over that of anyone else. She'd constantly been at his side as he conducted business with other men. She'd traveled with him throughout Europe, to India, and even on a harrowing sea voyage to the islands in the Caribbean. As a result, she'd learned to judge people by their words and actions, and by their character.

Her unique upbringing showed itself when she was old enough to participate in the social events of London's Season. She was different from other young women her age. She was never one to become starry-eyed or tongue-tied at the sight of a handsome face. She preferred the engagement of lively conversation.

This, naturally, created confusion. Most men of her age and social class were not comfortable with a female who expected to be treated as an equal. And women thought her strange, as well. Different.

It occurred to her now that perhaps this explained Rosa's attitude.

In any event, no man anywhere near her age had fascinated her enough to capture her attention. And now, here she was, impressed by this stranger.

The Rainbow's proprietor stole up to the table like a lioness on the hunt and asked if they were being taken care of. Timour stood, thanked her, and smiled. When the woman moved away, Pearl was certain she heard an audible sigh of pleasure. Before she reached her counter, she barked at their waiter to see to their table first.

Pearl touched the petals of the blue flowers, thinking that she knew exactly how the woman felt.

"They are beautiful...like you."

Her face caught fire as his intense dark eyes fixed on her. She immediately searched for something to say.

"I'd love to learn more about the Book of Kings you mentioned earlier."

"The *Shahnameh*."

"Yes, can you tell me about the story? The one that makes everyone cry."

"The story of Rustam and Sohrab?"

"Yes."

"Do you enjoy tragedies?"

"I do."

"What are some that you are particularly fond of?"

"I've read and reread Shakespeare's plays."

"All of them?"

Pearl had never been good at lying. And right now, what difference did it make if what she told him was the whole truth or a part of it? Her troubles were her own secrets to keep. But she could surely speak freely of her education and her interests. After all, they were simply two strangers, brought together for a few hours. No shared past. No shared future.

"Yes. All of them."

"Anyone else's work?"

She and her father had to part with everything they'd owned when the creditors showed up at their house to take possession. Losing the house and furniture and jewelry and wardrobes of clothing had not hurt as much as losing their well-stocked library.

"I have a rather tearstained copy of Goethe's *Sorrows of Young Werther*."

It was one of the dozen volumes Pearl had been able to hold onto. She'd carried it in a satchel to Marshalsea.

"And who does not?"

A smile pulled at her lip, but she said nothing more as the server approached and slid two platters of food onto the table along with forks and knives.

"What is the story of Rustam and Sohrab about?" she asked when he left them.

"Let us eat while I decide if I can relate a shortened version of it. One that will not do irreparable harm to the original work."

They ate in a comfortable silence, chatting occasionally about the food and the other patrons. It appeared that the coffee house was preparing to close, though no one was hurrying them.

When the meal had been cleared away, Pearl watched him tap his long fingers on the table. She sensed that he was traveling through the world of the story she'd asked him to relate.

She didn't press him. Finally, he turned in his seat toward her, his dark eyes again capturing her gaze. "Are you ready?"

"I am. Are you?"

His smile was like sunshine warming a January day.

"Rustam was a warrior, a hero to his people, well known throughout the land. Then one day, unforeseen circumstances stranded him in a foreign country."

"What circumstances?"

"His horse was stolen."

"Where? How?"

"He was sleeping, and some soldiers took the horse. So, he followed them."

"On foot?"

He leaned toward her, the wrinkles reappearing at the corners of his eyes. "I will be glad to recite the long version for you, Miss Smith. But that means we shall need to remain in each other's company longer than either of us had planned."

A lovely warmth spread through her body. She wet her lips. "I apologize for the interruptions. Please continue."

"While Rustam was visiting this neighboring country, he became the guest of the king. There at court, he met a beautiful maiden named Tehmina. And the two of them took an immediate liking to each other."

The tale sounded suspiciously similar to their situation. But Pearl kept the observation to herself.

"Now, if they got married or not that first night has been the subject of eight hundred years of debate."

"Wait! So, it was a case of love at first sight?"

He nodded. "She went to his bedchamber, and they spent the night together."

"Oh!" Pearl felt the blush rise into her face, and she was happy for the dimness of the light shed by the lamps on the walls.

"The version I prefer is that Rustam was smitten by the beautiful and wise Tehmina. He sent a message to the king that they desired to be married. The king was happy with the development, and a lavish traditional marriage was arranged for them."

There were many questions she had for him, but recalling his playful threat, she forced herself to wait.

"Rustam stayed in Samangan for a while."

"Is that the name of the country?"

"Yes. He still needed to find his horse."

"What about his wife?"

"He spent many loving nights and days with Tehmina."

Her mind lingered on the meaning of 'loving nights' for a few heartbeats longer than it should have. "Did he find his horse?"

"Eventually, he found his great war horse. Soon after, he realized that it was time for him to leave."

Pearl frowned, already knowing and accepting that there would be an end to this night, too. Timour would leave. And she had to return to her life and the hopelessness of the troubles plaguing her and her father. Her fingers again reached for the blue flowers on the table, touching the tender pedals. Tomorrow, they would begin to wither and fade.

"Are you certain you want to hear more?"

"Yes, of course." She turned her attention back to him.

"When Rustam told Tehmina about his departure, she revealed that she was carrying their child. He was overjoyed at this news, but he still had to go."

Pearl sat back in the chair, her hands clutched on her lap. Timour had warned her beforehand that this was a tragedy.

"Before he left, he gave Tehmina a precious jewel. He requested that if the baby was a girl, she tie it in the child's hair. If it was a boy, she should have him wear it on his upper arm. Then, with a heavy heart, Rustam mounted his horse and bade her a tearful farewell."

A server approached, but Pearl waved him away. She wanted to hear more, even though she was sure that what followed would not end happily.

"Please go on."

"Years passed. Rustam was unaware that he had a son by Princess Tehmina."

"She was a princess?"

"She was. But more important, she was independent. She had immense courage and spoke her mind."

Timour's gaze kept Pearl under a spell. She couldn't look away if she tried. Each word was spoken as if they were meant to compliment *her*.

"What did Tehmina name the son?"

"Sohrab."

The servers were noisily putting benches and chairs up on the tables, and she realized that they were the only patrons remaining.

"I believe they're trying to tell us something," she said, picking up her flowers.

"You are correct." He stood and placed two coins on the table. "Am I paying them too much?"

Pearl handed him one of the coins back. "Leaving just this, you will no doubt be their most cherished customer."

When they were again in the open air and walking down toward the Strand, she took a deep breath and looked up at him.

"Rustam and Sohrab. This is not going to end well, is it?"

10

———

THEY TURNED west and made their way along the wide street she'd referred to as the Strand. The clanging of bells from boats on the river occasionally reached them as they walked, and the moon was a white disk in the sky.

They passed businesses of all kinds that lined the thoroughfare—from printing houses to millinery and clothing shops to tea and chop houses. The eating and drinking establishments were all open and busy, and the streets were filled here, as well, with carriages, pedestrians, and vendors.

"Will you tell me the rest of the story?"

Timour glanced at Pearl's beautiful face, glowing beneath the light of street lamps.

The epic poems of the *Shahnameh* were a part of every Iranian's education. It was a pillar of their history and culture. Regardless of their wealth or place in society, everyone knew the stories, and most could recite lines and even long sections of the poems word for word. The tales were told and retold by parents, by teachers in the schools, by mullahs in the houses of worship. Quranic study groups and Sufi dervishes all used the text quite often as a starting point for philosophical and spiritual debate.

He was touched that Pearl cared to hear the rest of the story.

"Where was I?"

"Tehmina had a son named Sohrab, and Rustam was gone."

He picked up the tale from there. "Years passed without the father and son ever meeting. But the child grew, and Sohrab became a strong and skilled warrior. And he was young and made the mistakes of the young."

There were always those wolves at court who benefited themselves at the expense of an ambitious youth. Timour knew too much about court life.

"What did he do?"

"Unaware of the ways of the world and overconfident about his strength and ability, he declared that he would raise an army, defeat the king of Iran, and make his father and mother king and queen."

"So Sohrab knew his father was Rustam?"

"It was no secret. Although they had never met, he had heard many stories from his mother of Rustam's prowess as a warrior."

"And could he do it? Could Sohrab raise an army?"

"There were many self-serving wolves in the court who helped him. They were men who had ambitions of their own."

"And he attacked the country?"

"He was quite successful. The epic gives an impressive account of his victories. Of how he built his reputation. He grew even stronger and more formidable until there was no one brave enough to challenge him."

A dismayed frown clouded her face. "Except Rustam."

"Yes. The poet Ferdowsi tells us that the king of Iran lured Rustam back from retirement. He sent him to do battle against this new enemy."

"Father and son. Facing each other."

"And neither knew the identity of the other."

"Oh, no."

"Shall I stop?"

"No, no. Please continue."

"Rustam was reluctant to go into battle. But kings have their own plans and ways to get what they want." No one knew that better than Timour himself. "In the days before the battle, the two foes first took stock of each other. Then they met in single combat, and Sohrab nearly bests Rustam several times. Strangely, respect and affection begin to grow within him. On impulse, he asks if the aging warrior is Rustam. The father denies it, saying he is a far weaker figure than the great hero."

"He lies to Sohrab?"

"Rustam doesn't know that he's fighting his son. After many days of battle, he is weakening. His intention is to win, and he doesn't want to give his young enemy more incentive. Duel after duel they fight, and Sohrab asks again. Each time the father denies the truth. Until..."

"Until?" She stopped, facing him.

"In their last day of battle, Rustam wrestles Sohrab to the ground, stabbing him fatally."

Her hand went to her mouth. "No!"

"As the lifeblood drains from him, Sohrab tells the great warrior how his love for his father—the mighty hero Rustam—brought him there in the first place. Rustam, to his horror, realizes the truth. Stripping away Sohrab's armor, he finds his own jewel on his dying son's arm. But he has learned the truth too late. He has killed his own son."

Tears glistened in Pearl's eyes as she wrapped her arms around her middle. "So sad. A father killing his own child."

Timour wanted to gather her in his arms but fought the impulse. Propriety stopped him.

"What happened to Tehmina?" she asked after a moment.

"When she finds out her son is dead, she burns Sohrab's house and gives away all of his riches. Then, as Ferdowsi puts it, 'the breath departed from her body, and her spirit went forth after Sohrab her son.'"

She turned around, but not before Timour saw the tears fall.

He watched her. Others on the street walked past them with hushed voices and curious stares. Timour saw only Pearl. He thought of nothing but how quickly his attraction to her was growing. She was genuine. Her emotions were real. She was affected deeply by the legend. As was every Iranian man, woman, and child upon first hearing the tale. She was a rare gem.

"I am sorry that I have made you cry."

She ran her fingers under her eyes and turned around, smiling. "You warned me. I should have known."

He offered her his arm, and she took it as they started off again.

They followed the Strand, which now curved gently to the right, and he knew from her face that she was contemplating the story. He was glad she'd responded to the tale as she had; it had always been an important one for him. Perhaps it was because Timour was part of a line of kings and nobles whose history was captured in those stories. But, like Sohrab, he'd always struggled against the preordained path that had been laid out for him. It was a path decided upon by courtiers.

The advisors to his father had wanted him to have a career in the army; he was fond of literature. They had asked him to live in Tabriz; he preferred the life and art and bustle of Isfahan. Marriages were arranged for his brothers in their youth; Timour had resisted. But here he was in London; finally forced to go through with a marriage of diplomacy. This time, his father hadn't relied on advisors; he'd asked him directly. Timour had no choice but to agree.

He thought of Ferdowsi's work. What if Sohrab had never become a warrior. Never left his country to follow his own dream. He would have lived out his life in peace and boredom. He would have died an old man, untested and forgotten. It didn't matter that taking his destiny into his own hands brought danger. It also brought the reward of immortality in the words of a timeless poem.

They reached a wide intersection of streets and lanes, and passed a large old coaching inn called the Golden Cross, which looked like it had seen better days. In the center of the crossroads, a statue of regal-looking figure on horseback stood guard over the neighborhood, himself protected by a wrought iron fence.

"Charles the First. His story didn't turn out happily either, I can tell you that."

"Oh, yes. His arrogance cost him his head, if I recall the history."

"Are all of the tales in the Shahnameh as tragic?"

"Rustam and Sohrab is the most tragic. Others will move you and thrill you, but none are as heart wrenching."

"I want to read them. All of them. Have they been translated into other languages than English?"

"Louis-Mathieu Langlès, the French academic and philosopher, has translated some of the episodes into French."

"I shall look for them."

"Thank you for confirming that you speak French." He smiled down at her.

"Since we're again delving into the truth about each other, how is it that you know so much about every academic and philosopher, living and dead? How is it that you know precisely who is translating Persian literature?"

Since the *Shahnameh*'s inception, every king who ruled Iran commissioned the production of a new copy of the epic poem. Renowned artists and calligraphers competed for the opportunity to be chosen. Timour was the member of the royal family in charge of deciding on the artists for the next edition.

"Because I am simply fond of reading?"

Pearl quirked an eyebrow skeptically.

"I am deeply wounded that you do not believe me, Miss Smith."

She scoffed. "Not too deeply, I think."

"Is this Pall Mall?" he asked as a distraction. The road stretched out straight and level to the west.

"Yes, it is. The Prince Regent himself has a residence up ahead." She gestured to a long row of buildings that were being taken down on the right side. "These houses are being removed to make the street wider."

"Change is constant," he remarked. "Do you resist change, Miss Smith?"

"It depends."

"On what?"

"On whether I have a say in it or not. Too often, we have no choice in what life hands us, in where it takes us." She rubbed her arms and stepped away. "And this is a new gallery that has recently opened."

As she continued to point out the sights, Timour found himself paying less attention to the history than to her well masked sorrow. She put up a front of wit and humor, but behind it she was hurting.

She was also unlike any woman he'd ever met or spent time with. She voiced her opinions about people without hesitation. She had firm opinions about the wrongs inflicted by the strong on the weak. She mentioned several times the injustice of building great wealth at the expense of the poor.

"I'd have to say that your French education is showing

itself," he said with a smile after she made a comment about the Prince Regent's lavish renovating of Buckingham Castle to make it a palace. "You sound almost revolutionary in your ideas."

"I don't mean to offend you. I simply think it's wrong to take the possessions of others by force."

"I am not offended, at all. The European empires are expanding, and nations are fighting to control more and more of the world. No one seems concerned with the fact that you cannot silence hungry and desperate people for long. And the point of a bayonet or the barrage of a cannon will never earn someone's love."

"I agree with you whole-heartedly." She sighed and then looked around her. "But I would remind you that you're now in England where we busily concoct plots and evidence to ensnare people, put them behind bars, and seize their livelihoods."

Timour glanced at the seriousness of her profile. Pearl wasn't speaking in general terms. He got a strong sense she was talking about her own situation in some way.

"And we do the same thing abroad," she continued, warming to the topic. "Not a mile from here, the British Museum has an entire library of rare, antique manuscripts that we have stolen from lands we are exploiting in other ways. There are ancient works from Egypt, Greece, Rome, and from Ottoman lands. I wouldn't be surprised if they have rare copies of the *Shahnameh*, as well."

Timour wouldn't have been surprised, either.

"When I was in India," she continued, growing more

indignant. "An officer of the British East India Company was crowing about a recent acquisition of an ancient text that they were able to 'steal' from a local rajah. His very words. A common, everyday occurrence over there."

"You have been to India. There is no end to your surprises, Miss Smith. Next, I shall learn that you have a residence near my home in Isfahan."

"I...I only..." Her dark eyes rounded and then sparkled with amusement.

An older woman, accompanied by a young man in uniform, stepped into their path and put her hand on Pearl's arm.

"Miss Smith? I thought my eyes was betraying me, but it *is* you, Miss Smith."

Timour noticed how Pearl's face had gone pale, but she didn't pull away from the woman.

"Oh my dear, what pleasure it is to run into you. My sweet Miss Smith. Frank, you recall this precious lady, don't you?"

"I do." The soldier bowed.

"I was just telling him how sick with worry I've been about you and your father of late. I didn't know if—"

"Hush. Hush, my dear Mrs. Johnson." Pearl turned to Timour. "Will you forgive me for a moment, sir. I need a moment."

He bowed and walked away a few paces to give them privacy. Mrs. Johnson was well-dressed, but not in the overly opulent manner of the women he'd seen going into the ball. But they clearly knew one another well—they stood holding hands like dear friends—but the reunion had upset Pearl for some reason.

Gradually, more and more about Pearl Smith was coming to light. And all the things he was guessing were proving to be accurate.

11

"FRANK IS in the army now, my dear. He has just returned from the Peninsula, thank the Lord."

"I'm glad to see you safely home, Frank."

She was all too aware of Timour's eyes on them. Mrs. Johnson had been the housekeeper in their Berkeley Square home for all of Pearl's life. Right after her father's arrest, she'd made a point of visiting the efficient and kindhearted woman, settling her salary with what little money of her own she had left. But that was last winter. She hadn't seen her since.

"Where are you living now?"

There was no way she could admit the truth. "Staying with a friend."

"How is your dear father faring in that horrible place?"

Pearl's throat closed, and all she could do was nod.

"Do you go to see him often?"

"I do, yes."

"But how are you, my child? You look pale to me. And you're so thin."

"I'm very well, Mrs. Johnson. Thank you."

"But what is this dress you're wearing? And you're out without so much as a bonnet."

The older woman was abrupt, to be sure, but Pearl could never take offense. The concern was motherly and protective. Their housekeeper had nothing but affection in her heart for them.

"Perhaps I could stop by for a visit soon?" Pearl suggested. "We can chat about all that is happening in the world."

"Of course. But now that the house is all closed up, I can come and tend to your needs. I'll work only during the day if your friend hasn't a spare room for me."

"We can certainly talk about it when I call on you."

Mrs. Johnson's eyes drifted toward the flowers in Pearl's hand. "My dearest one. I can see you need someone to look after you. I can only imagine what you've been through, how you've suffered. You don't need to worry about paying me."

The grandson discreetly took a step back and made a production of busying himself looking at his pocket watch.

Emotions welled up in Pearl's throat, threatening to choke her. "Thank you. Let's wait to discuss that."

"Your father is a good and honest man. But do you have any prospects of his friends paying his debts and getting him out of that horrible Marshalsea?"

"I'll never give up hope," Pearl croaked.

"That's the spirit. But how will you do it?" Mrs. Johnson

cast a quick look at where Timour stood. "Would Mr. Smith approve?"

Pearl could only imagine what was running through the old woman's mind. Here she was, walking unchaperoned. Late at night. With a stranger. And carrying flowers.

"Yes, he would. You have nothing to fear, Mrs. Johnson. Mr. Mirza is a gentleman and a trusted friend. He has been kind enough to walk with me to Lord and Lady Whitwell's house."

"Oh! Lovely! Yes, of course. Tonight is the ball. I'm sure that all of your old friends are there." She leaned in, lowering her voice. "I'm so glad that you were invited."

Pearl wasn't going to correct her.

"But you're not dressed for the event, my dear. And you're going on foot? At this hour?"

"It's a costume ball, Mrs. Johnson. I was there earlier, but I was called away. But now, I really must go." She threw a glance in the direction of Timour, hinting that she was inconveniencing him by standing and talking. Which she probably was. "Please excuse me."

"Of course. Of course. But promise that you'll come and take tea with me this week. Will you?"

Pearl nodded and backed away, bidding Frank goodbye, as well.

The housekeeper and her grandson proceeded toward Haymarket, and Pearl breathed a sigh of relief. As much as she cared for their former housekeeper, she was anxious to get away from them.

Meeting these two people accomplished one thing for

sure. It shook her awake. These few enjoyable hours this evening had been an indulgence in fantasy. Now, reality slithered grimly toward Pearl from the darkness, clutching at her with sharp, inescapable claws.

It was impossible to run away from her past or present life, and she couldn't bear the thought of answering questions Timour must have. He had remained motionless for the entire time she was speaking to Mrs. Johnson.

She avoided his gaze now, saying in a rush, "I'm grateful for dinner and the pleasure of your company, Mr. Mirza. But I *must* get back to Whitwell House."

"As you wish. I shall walk back with you."

"No. That won't be necessary." The knot in her throat was growing larger. "If you are not needed at the ball, there is a great deal to see and do in London. A hackney cab can take you across the river to Vauxhall. The pleasure gardens are a delight. And now, if you will forgive me, I shall bid you adieu."

Pearl dropped a quick curtsy and started down the sidewalk, half walking, half running. She had no plan as to where she was actually going. Returning to Whitwell House was not the best option, considering her escape from the cloak room. She could only imagine how Rosa had received word of her leaving. And there was no point in going all the way to Marshalsea. The areas she'd be walking through on the other side of the river were dangerous after dark, and the prison gates would not open for her until dawn.

Still, she had to get away.

"Miss Smith."

Embarrassment gripped her as Timour caught up and fell

in step with her. "Please, Mr. Mirza. I have nothing to say. No explanation that I'm willing to provide."

"Did I ask anything of you?"

He hadn't.

"Your business is yours. I shall not intrude."

His assurance should have calmed her, but instead her emotions surged to the surface. She looked away, her vision blurry with tears.

"You are shivering. If I may?"

She felt the weight of his coat drape over her shoulders. As she continued to hurry on, she dashed away tears but still tasted them on her lips.

Mrs. Johnson had asked about prospects and friends. Her father had none. Pearl had imagined she was strong enough to face the seemingly insurmountable odds against them. She'd told herself that she would never give up. But that was yesterday. That was when she still clung to the vague hope that Lord Castlereagh would intervene on their behalf. No more. That possibility had been crushed this evening.

"Could we sit for a moment...over there, perhaps?"

Timour was not giving up. She looked away as her tears continued to fall.

"If you please, Miss Smith."

He was gesturing toward St. James's Square, beyond an open lot where a house had recently stood. Newly installed gaslit street lamps illuminated the streets and walks surrounding the square.

His hand touched her back, and he guided her to a bench. Within a wrought iron fence, an equestrian statue of William of Orange had been erected in the center of the wide circular pool. The moon and the soft breeze created a show of magical, glistening light on the surface of the water.

Pearl put her flowers down on the bench next to her and raised her face to the cool air. She closed her eyes and tried to calm her thoughts and her emotions, with little success. The situation she and her father were in was dire. And she didn't know where to turn next. Whom to ask for help. They sat in silence for a time.

Finally, Timour spoke. "When God wishes to help, he lets us weep. Wherever water flows, life flourishes. Wherever tears fall, divine mercy is shown."

His quiet words pierced the nagging feeling of despair within her, and she turned to her companion. "That is beautiful. You're a poet, as well?"

"I wish I could take credit for those lines. They are words of the great Persian poet, Jalal ad-Din Muhammad Rumi."

"Another long name I shall need to memorize."

"We call him Mulana. Perhaps that is easier for you to remember."

"Mulana," she repeated. "Is he from the same time as Ferdowsi?"

"Later. He was born only six centuries ago."

"Oh, practically a contemporary of ours."

"The wisdom of our poets is timeless."

"And *your* wisdom to have read their work and memorized it," she said softly. "You share their words, their art, where it is needed. You know what to say and how to act in every situation, it seems."

He shook off her compliment. "If I were a better man—a man of greater wisdom, perhaps—I would have already acted to wash away your troubles and heal your sadness. I would have used my bare hands, if necessary, to set to right the wrongs that afflict you. I would have replaced your tears with smiles."

Pearl placed her hand on top of his. "Thank you, Mr. Mirza. You are the kindest person I've met in a dreadfully long time."

His strong fingers closed around hers. "You should not suffer like this. Is there anything I can do for you? Anything at all?"

Pearl thought of how—during the few hours spent in this man's company—she'd felt a temporary reprieve from the harsh judgments of life. She'd felt...happiness.

She turned slightly on the bench to face him. "After tonight, each of us will go our separate way. So there is something."

"Ask and it will be granted."

"If only for a few moments, could you share more of the poetry of Ferdowsi and Mulana with me?"

Timour's laughter rang through the night, then his eyes met hers, as if he didn't believe her. "I offer you the moon, and this is what you ask."

"We already share the moon and the stars. Poetry is all I long for now."

12

DAWN WAS BREAKING across the London sky, and the city to the east of them was crowned with streaks of gold. When Timour and Pearl noticed the lamplighter who came by to extinguish the streetlights casting disparaging looks in their direction, they ceased their discussion of literature and life and roused themselves from their bench. Carts loaded with meats and produce rolled past them on their way to the back alleys of the stately homes. The delivery men, already weary from their labors, barely looked at them at all.

They walked up to Piccadilly, where the morning traffic was lighter than it had been last night. When she tried to take her leave of him there, a mild dispute broke out between them whether it was safe for her to walk home alone. Finally, Pearl submitted to his demand that she ride in a passing hackney cab. She was given no opportunity to object as Timour paid the driver enough money to carry her to Bath and back again if she chose.

"Perhaps we shall see each other again soon, Miss Smith," Timour told her before the carriage departed.

Pearl shook her head, feeling a pang of sadness. "I shall forever cherish the memory of this night—of you and the poetry of your country. But my life is not my own. My world is filled with trouble and my future is a tangle of thorns. Believe me when I say that I wish you well, but this is where we must say goodbye."

"Mulana says, 'If you want the moon, do not hide from the night. If you want a rose, do not run from the thorns.' I will only say...until next time."

Timour's words stayed with her as the cab rolled through London streets. The time they'd spent in each other's company had been brief, but Pearl's heart, her mind, her entire being had been touched by him.

If you want a rose, do not run from the thorns.

He gave her permission to dream. To think of herself as worthy was a gift she was desperate for, and he'd given it to her.

I will only say...until next time.

Pearl had no doubt that for the rest of her life, wherever she went, she'd be searching for him. Daring to hope that they'd one day meet again.

After returning to Marshalsea, she found her father awake and waiting for her. He was under the impression that she'd stayed with a friend last night. He was happy to hear of her accidental meeting with their old housekeeper. She left out any mention of her Persian companion.

All morning, Pearl's mind did not stray far from Timour. The previous evening took on a dreamlike quality for her. She recalled the way the moon cast its light and shadows around them. She saw his handsome face and heard the passion in his voice as he retold the legends and recited the poetry of his land. She felt again the warmth of his kindness and the strength of his character.

At the same time, her heart beat leadenly from the knowledge that the evening they spent together would be all they'd ever have.

After the bells of the city tolled the noon hour, her father settled down to read, and Pearl left him. She wouldn't allow herself to mope about when she had so much to do. The confrontation in the cloakroom last night had closed off an avenue for her and her father, and now she needed to walk and consider some other path to pursue.

Working for Rosa was behind her, but Pearl was still owed money for her past work. Determined to get it, she set off for Park Lane to see the housekeeper and settle their account.

An hour later, she entered Londonderry House and found out that everyone in the Servants' Hall had apparently been given the task of notifying their mistress if Pearl were to show up.

"She wants to see you, miss. You're to wait here," a lady's maid told her before running for the stairs to inform Rosa.

Pearl stood alone, ignoring the stares of the servants passing by. Coming here, day after day, had accomplished nothing to help her father. She'd been foolish to imagine these people would suddenly find compassion. There was nothing in the world that would move Lord Castlereagh to respond any differently than his niece had done.

Before seeking out Rosa, Pearl had earned some money tutoring young daughters of a number of merchants in the vicinity of the prison. As she'd walked across Blackfryars Bridge, she'd decided she would go back to that work. With a few more students, she'd be able to earn enough for their survival. More importantly, she wouldn't have to face any of the unpleasantness of dealing with the likes of Rosa Cly.

The servant returned, breathless from running. "She'll see you in her sitting room."

Pearl went up the back stairs to Rosa's apartments. Taking a deep breath, she knocked on the door and entered. This time, her former 'friend' was alone.

"I must say, Pearl. I'm seriously displeased with you." Rosa stood by the fireplace and planted one hand on her hip. "In the name of charity, I ask you to come to the Whitwell House, and what do you do? You besmirch my good name, abandoning your post the first chance you get. In leaving the cloakroom unattended, you embarrassed Lady Whitwell to no end. And you betrayed me entirely."

A thousand objections rose up inside of Pearl, but she forced herself to remain silent. She wanted this meeting to be as short as possible, but Rosa's tirade continued. She went on to list the name of every person who'd come to the cloakroom and failed to receive help. She related every supposed conversation with the multitude of appalled guests who were so shockingly treated. Finally, as if the event rivaled the fall of Troy, Rosa dramatized the traumatic moment when she had to apologize to Lady Whitwell.

As she listened, Pearl found herself wondering how long Rosa had rehearsed this tragic soliloquy. Finally, she couldn't take it anymore.

"Stop. I came today to collect what you owe me. You no longer need to suffer because of me."

"I'm not through with you." Clearly horrified at having been interrupted, Rosa took a step toward her. "You have proved to be a terrible disappointment to me."

"And you to me, Rosa."

"*Rosa*? How dare you refer to me in such an informal manner. I am Miss Cly to you. *Never* forget that. And as far as this supposed pittance you say I owe, I'd say you have forfeited any claim to it."

She stopped at the sound of a knock on the door. Without taking her hard gaze from Pearl's face, she called out for the person to enter.

It was the butler. "I'm sorry to intrude, Miss Cly. Your uncle has just arrived with company. He's asked that you come down to the library immediately."

Rosa pointed a threatening finger at Pearl. "I'm not finished with you. Go to the Servants' Hall and wait for me to send for you."

But *she* was finished with Rosa and this household, Pearl thought. Whatever wages she was owed, it was not worth listening to any more of this.

"I'm afraid his lordship has asked for Miss Smith to come to the library, as well," the butler said.

"Whatever for?"

"I cannot say, Miss Cly."

He barely had time to get out of the way as Rosa swept out of the room.

"Would you care to have me show you the way, Miss Smith?" the man asked politely.

"No, I remember." She'd been in Londonderry House as a guest many times.

"Very good, miss. I suggest you take the main stairs."

As she descended the stairs, Pearl thought of how long she'd prayed for this chance. But now that she was about to be in Lord Castlereagh's company, she had no hope. She already knew what the answer would be.

At the door of the library, a servant announced her. Lord Castlereagh himself, tall and thin as a broomstick, left his niece's side and crossed the room to greet her.

He bowed. "My dear Miss Smith. It's been far too long."

"My lord." Pearl curtsied, shocked by the greeting. She'd already expected Rosa to have spewed venom about her in the few moments between their arrival. "You're too kind."

Rosa stood in the center of the library, trying to look calm and composed, but her eyes were locked on something else in the room.

Pearl followed her gaze to a cluster of chairs by the window, and her heart leapt in her chest. Timour, dressed in an elegant gray coat, detailed with braided cord and gleaming gold, bowed to her.

He was as handsome as the image of him that she carried in her mind. But a dozen questions burned on her tongue. What was he doing here? She recalled him asking about Rosa in the courtyard last night. Did he know her? And what was his connection with Lord Castlereagh?

"I understand that you already know Prince Timour Mirza of Persia, Miss Smith."

Prince. Her mouth turned dry, and heat rose from her neck into her cheeks. For a moment, she thought she might faint. Timour's handsome dark eyes were only on her, and an enigmatic smile pulled at his lips.

She curtsied again, this time much deeper. "Your Royal Highness."

Castlereagh took Pearl by the arm. "Come and join us, Miss Smith. There is a great deal that I need to say to you."

He guided her to where the royal guest waited. Pearl couldn't tear her eyes from the prince. A *prince*. Their conversation last night should have given her some clue. The scope of his knowledge. His confidence. His generosity.

His eyes spoke to her. He'd said *until next time*, and now he was here.

Rosa, ever the obedient niece, followed them to the group of chairs, and they all sat down.

"This morning, His Royal Highness brought the unfortunate matter of your good father to my attention."

Pearl's gaze moved to Timour again. He was seated across from her. How did he know? The only thing she could think of was that he'd overheard her conversation with Mrs. Johnson. She choked up. He'd tried to have her reveal her troubles. But she wouldn't.

"I have been entirely remiss with regard to his situation," Lord Castlereagh continued. "Though I must ask for your understanding of my negligence. This war with France has required all of my attention."

The words struggled to get past her lips. But she forced herself to say them. "Of course, my lord."

Rosa stared red-faced at her hands.

"Nonetheless, it is a grave matter involving an old friend. And I should have seen to its resolution much sooner."

Pearl was unable to believe what she was hearing. *Resolution*? She stared at Lord Castlereagh's sincere expression. The man appeared to mean what he said.

"The good news is that at this very moment, my clerk should be arriving at Marshalsea to obtain your father's release. The Foreign Office will see to any outstanding debts."

"Thank you." She found herself on her feet. "Thank you, my lord. But I should go there at once. I must attend to my father. He'll be so grateful. But I must see to living arrangements. I really must go."

Everyone rose to their feet.

"If you find it agreeable, Miss Smith..." It was the first time Timour had spoken since she entered the room. "I have directed my ambassador to prepare one of the royal apartments at the embassy for you and Mr. Smith. My cousin, Ali Khan, will see to every detail of the move from your current residence."

The man certainly had a way of taking her breath away. Pearl felt like she was floating on a cloud.

"And now, if you will excuse me, Lord Castlereagh. I would like to escort Miss Smith to meet with her father."

"Of course, Your Highness. I hope you will be able to dine with us tomorrow, as we'd planned?"

"I shall have my cousin confirm with your office the new schedule for the remainder of my stay in your fine city."

"Your new schedule. Of course."

Pearl was unaware of having left the mansion until a footman opened the door of an impressive brougham waiting in front of Londonderry House. Timour handed her in and took the seat facing her.

"Your Highness, I am...I am..." She tried to find the right words. Her heart pounded in her chest. Now, within the confines of the carriage, she was too shy to look him in the eye. He was a miracle worker. A handsome, loving man who had descended like an angel into her path. He was giving her another chance at life. "How can my father and I ever repay you for all you've done."

"I have already been paid, Miss Smith. A thousand times over."

"How is that even possible?"

"I was sent here to London on a mission of diplomacy. Unfortunately, I allowed myself to be induced to go beyond what is necessary. Meeting you has allowed me to correct the situation."

"I don't understand."

"My country is signing a treaty with England. Its purpose

is to block any chance of Russian threats to British holdings in India. In addition to this agreement, this government has insisted that I take an English wife."

Pearl remembered the conversation she'd overheard outside of Rosa's room. "And that wife is to be Rosa Cly?"

"Her or someone like her, if the Foreign Office has its way. But I am no longer willing to accept that."

"What about the treaty?"

He scoffed. "You've been to India. It is far too valuable to England. Do you think my refusal to marry would stop them from signing these papers?"

She didn't think so, but what did she know about these things. "I'm still unclear about my part in any of this."

"Well, this is what I am hoping your part will be." He leaned forward and took her hand. "For the next month, you and your father will be my guests. Afterwards, I am hoping that your father will agree to accompany me to Iran. The import and manufacture of textiles will need someone with his expertise."

"I...I don't know what to say, except that I know he'll be beside himself."

"And I was hoping you will agree to accompany us, as well."

"Of course. I would be delighted."

His thumb gently caressed the back of her hand. She looked from their joined hands to his handsome face.

"There, I can introduce you to my father, my brothers and sisters, and their families."

"That will be lovely." She smiled. Her heart began to beat

even faster. "And I promise to learn the entire name of each of them before I'm introduced."

Timour laughed. "That is an excellent way to begin."

"Where shall we start? What is the first name I should learn?"

"Names." His eyes fell on her lips. "A pair of them, I think."

"A pair of names." Pearl inched toward him, hoping he would kiss her.

"I am Hazrat-e Ajal Shahzadeh Timour Mirza. You are Banoo Pearl Smith."

"Wait. Wait. Did you just give me a title?"

"Of course. The prince's wife must always have a title."

———

FOR MORE MAY McGoldrick historical romance, try their award-winning, full-length novel Borrowed Dreams, *Book 1 of the Pennington Family series.*

If you enjoyed *A Prince in the Pantry*, please consider telling your friends or posting a short review. Word of mouth is an author's best friend...and much appreciated.

And before you go, take a look at the preview of **Borrowed Dreams** that we've included at the end of this book.

AUTHORS' NOTE

FOR THOSE READERS who have been following our stories, you know that we cheerfully jump from novels set in the Scottish Highlands to London and from the Middle Ages to the Regency and beyond. We hope you are enjoying the variety in the tales and the characters we create.

For our new readers, we wanted to thank you for sharing in a story that we have been dying to tell for some time now. As always, we have tried to depict a place and a time in a way that mingles the real and the imagined in an entertaining way. Berkeley Square and Covent Garden and Regency Park are, of course, actual places. And for the characters in *A Prince in the Pantry*, we drew from Nikoo's Qajar ancestors, who ruled Iran for centuries.

Looking forward, the preview that is included at the end of this book is *Borrowed Dreams*, the first installment of the Pennington Family series. In that award winning novel, a wonderful woman named Millicent Wentworth, who was introduced to readers in *The Promise*, has a second chance at happiness with the notorious and badly wounded 'Lord of Scandal', Lyon Pennington, Earl of Aytoun. Reviewers have referred to this as a fresh twist on the Beauty and Beast tale.

Prequels to the Pennington Family Series

The Promise
The Rebel

———

Pennington Family Series: 1st Generation

In the Scottish Dream Trilogy, the Pennington Family series gets underway in *Borrowed Dreams* as three brothers struggle with the memory of Emma, an enigmatic young woman whose tragic and mysterious death at Baronsford Castle threatens to divide the family forever:

Borrowed Dreams
Captured Dreams
Dreams of Destiny

———

Pennington Family Series: 2nd Generation
Children of Millicent and Lyon

Romancing the Scot
It Happened in the Highlands
Sweet Home Highland Christmas *(novella)*
Sleepless in Scotland
Dearest Millie *(novella)*
How to Ditch a Duke *(novella)*

––––––––

As AUTHORS, we love feedback. We write our stories for our readers, and we'd love to hear from you. We are constantly learning, so please help us write stories that you will cherish and recommend to your friends. Please sign up for news and updates and follow us on BookBub.

Finally, if you liked *A Prince in the Pantry,* please leave a review online.

Visit us on our website - www.MayMcGoldrick.com

PREVIEW OF BORROWED DREAMS

A PENNINGTON FAMILY NOVEL

London

"We're going in the wrong direction, m'lady!"

Instead of turning west at the ancient Temple Bar, the carriage had turned east on Fleet Street, and the driver was now whipping his team through the busy traffic going into the City. The lawyer raised the head of his cane to the roof of the carriage to get the attention of the driver, but the touch of Millicent's gloved hand on his sleeve made him stop.

"He's going where he was directed, Sir Oliver. I have an urgent matter I need to see to at the wharves."

"At the wharves? But...but we're already somewhat pressed for time for your appointment, m'lady."

"This will not take very long."

He sank back against the seat, somewhat relieved. "Since we have a little time then, perhaps I could ask you a few questions about the secretive nature of this meeting we have been summoned to attend this morning."

"Please, Sir Oliver," Millicent pleaded quietly. "Can your questions wait until after my business at the wharves? I'm afraid my mind is rather distracted right now."

All his questions withered on the man's tongue as Lady Wentworth turned her face toward the window and the passing street scene. A short time later, the carriage passed by St. Paul's Cathedral and began wending its way down through a rough and odorous area in the direction of the Thames. By the time they crossed Fish Street, with its derelict sheds and warehouses, the lawyer could restrain himself no longer.

"Would you at least tell me the nature of this business at the wharves, m'lady?"

"We're going to an auction."

Oliver Birch looked out the window at the milling crowds of workmen and pickpockets and whores. "M'lady, I hope you intend to stay in the carriage and that you'll allow me to instruct one of the grooms to obtain what you're looking for."

"I'm sorry, sir, but it is essential that I see to this myself."

The lawyer grasped the side of the rocking carriage as the driver turned into the courtyard of a tumbledown wreck of a building on Brooke's Wharf. Outside the window, an odd mix of well-dressed gentlemen and shabby merchants and seamen stood in attendance on an auction that, from the looks of things, was already well under way.

"At least give me the details of what you intend to do here, Lady Wentworth." Birch climbed out of the carriage first. Despite the biting wind off the Thames, the smells of the place—combined with the stink of the river's edge—were appalling.

"I read about the auction in the *Gazette* this morning. They are selling off the estate of a deceased physician by the name of Dombey. The ruined man moved back from Jamaica last month." She pulled the hood up on her woolen cloak and accepted his hand as she stepped out. "Before he was put in debtor's prison, he succumbed to ill health some ten days ago."

Birch had to hurry to keep up with Millicent as she pushed her way through the crowd to the front row. "And what, may I ask, in Dr. Dombey's estate is of interest to you?"

She didn't answer, and the lawyer found his client's gray eyes searching anxiously past the personal articles that were laid out on a makeshift platform. "I hope I'm not too late."

The lawyer did not ask any more questions as Millicent's attention turned sharply toward the set of wide doors that led into the building. The bailiff was dragging out a frail-looking African woman wrapped in a tattered blanket and wearing only a dirty shift under it. A crate was placed on the platform, and the old woman—her neck and hands and feet in shackles—was pushed roughly onto it.

Birch closed his eyes for a moment to control his disgust at this evidence of the barbaric and dishonorable trade that continued to curse the nation…in spite of Lord Henley's comments that any slave stepping foot in England was free.

"Lookee, gennelmen. This here slave was Dr. Dombey's personal maid," the auctioneer shouted. "She's the only Negro the medical bloke carried back with him from Jamaica.

Aye, sure, she's a rum thing with her wrinkled face. And she's of an age to rival Methuselah. But gennelmen, she's said to be a weritable African queen, she is, and bright as crystal, they tell me. So e'en though she's worth a good thirty pounds, what say we start the bidding of at…at a pound."

There was loud jeering and laughter from the group.

"Look, now, gennelmen. 'Ow about ten shillings then?" the auctioneer announced over the roar of the crowd. "She's good teeth, she has." He pulled opened the woman's mouth roughly. There were crusts of blood on the chapped lips. "Ten shillings? Who'll start the bidding at ten shillings?"

"What bloody good is she?" somebody shouted.

"Five, gennelmen. Who'll start us at five?"

"The woman is nothing more than a refuse slave," another responded. "If we were in Port Royal, she'd be left to die on the wharf."

Birch glanced worriedly at Millicent and found a look of pain etched on her face. Tears were glimmering on the edges of her eyelids.

"This is no place for you to be, m'lady," he whispered quietly. "It is not right for you to be witnessing this. Whatever you came for must be already gone."

"The advertisement said she was a fine African lass." A middle-aged clerk, sneering from his place at the edge of the platform, threw a crumpled *Gazette* at the old woman. "Why, she's too old to even be good for—"

"Five pounds," Millicent called out.

Every eye in the place turned to her, and silence gripped the throng. Even the auctioneer seemed lost for words for a moment. Birch saw the woman's wrinkled eyelids open a fraction and stare at Millicent.

"Aye, yer ladyship. Yer bid is in fer—"

"Six pounds." A second bid from someone deep in the crowd silenced the auctioneer again. All heads in unison turned to the back of the auction yard.

"Seven," Millicent responded.

"Eight."

On the platform the man's face broke out into a grin as the crowds parted, showing a nattily dressed clerk holding up a rolled newspaper. "Why, I see Mr. Hyde's clerk is in attendance. Thank ye fer yer bid, Harry."

"Ten pounds," Millicent said with great vehemence.

Birch scanned the number of carriages in the yard, wondering from which one of them Jasper Hyde was issuing his commands. A large plantation owner in the West Indies and supposedly a good friend to the late Squire Wentworth, the Englishman had wasted no time in taking over all of the squire's properties in the Caribbean after his death in payment for debts Wentworth had owed him. And if that were not enough, since arriving in England, Mr. Hyde had positioned himself as Lady Wentworth's chief nemesis, buying up the rest of the bills of exchange and promissory notes the squire had left behind.

"Twenty."

There was a loud gasp of disbelief and the crowd began to shift uncomfortably.

"Thirty."

The lawyer turned to Millicent. "He's playing with you,

m'lady," he said quietly. "I don't believe it would be wise—"

"Fifty pounds," the clerk called without a trace of emotion.

A group of sailors near the edge of the platform turned and scoffed loudly at the clerk for pushing up the price.

"I can't let him do this. Dr. Dombey and this woman spent a great deal of time on Wentworth's plantations in Jamaica. From the stories I've heard from Jonah and some of the others at Melbury Hall, she became a person of some importance to them." She nodded to the auctioneer. "Sixty pounds."

Birch watched Jasper Hyde's clerk appear to squirm a little. The man turned and looked toward the line of carriages. The rolled newspaper rose in the air before the caller could repeat the last bid. "Seventy."

The rumbling in the crowd became more pronounced. There were sharp comments to the effect that he should let the woman have the slave. A couple of the sailors edged threateningly toward the clerk, muttering derisive obscenities.

"This is all a sick game to Mr. Hyde," Millicent whispered, turning away from the platform. "There are many stories of his brutality on the plantations. The stories about what he did after taking possession of my husband's land and slaves are even worse. He's answerable to no one and has no regard for what few laws are observed there. This woman has witnessed it all, though. He will hurt her. Kill her, perhaps." Her hands fisted. "Sir Oliver, I owe this to my people after all the suffering Wentworth caused. I can't in good conscience turn my back when I can save this one. Not when I've failed all those others that Hyde took."

"That it, yer ladyship?" the auctioneer asked. "Yer giving in?"

"Eighty," she replied, her voice quavering.

"You can't afford this, m'lady," Birch put in firmly but quietly. "Think of the promissory notes Hyde still holds from your husband. You've extended the date of repayment once. But they will all come due next month, and you are personally liable, to the extent of every last thing you own. And this includes Melbury Hall. You just can't add more fuel to his fire."

"One hundred pounds." The clerk's shout was instantly swallowed up by a loud response from the crowd. Birch watched the man take a few nervous steps toward the carriages as the same angry sailors moved closer to him.

"One ten, milady?" the auctioneer, grinning excitedly, called out from the platform.

"You can't save every one, Millicent," Birch whispered sharply. When first asked by the earl and the countess of Stanmore to represent Lady Wentworth in her legal affairs a year ago, he'd also been informed of the woman's great compassion for the Africans whom her late husband had held as slaves. But his expectations had not come close to the fervor he'd witnessed since then.

"I know that, Sir Oliver."

"For all we know, he might already own this woman. In the same way that he has been acquiring all of the late squire's notes, he may have done the same with Dombey. This may just be Jasper Hyde's way of draining the last of your available funds."

As his words sank in, Millicent's shoulders sagged. Wiping a tear from her face, she turned and started pushing her way toward the carriage. Halfway out of the yard, though, she swung around and raised a hand.

"One hundred ten."

A round of exclamations erupted from the crowd. Gradually, people parted until she was facing the pale-faced clerk across the mud and dirt of the yard. Having already retreated to back edge of the crowd, the man shook his head at the auctioneer and looked back at Millicent.

"Lady Wentworth can have her Negro at the price of a hundred ten pounds."

The mocking tones of the man, accompanied by his sneer, caused the sailors to lose the last of their restraint, and two took off after him. The clerk turned and bolted from the yard. Watching him run, Birch felt the urge to go after the clerk himself. There was no doubt in the lawyer's mind that this ordeal had been arranged. In a moment, the sailors returned empty-handed.

She laid her hand gently on his arm. "Regardless of Mr. Hyde's actions, I had to save this woman's life, Sir Oliver."

Millicent Gregory Wentworth could not be considered a great beauty, nor could her sense of style be called *au courant* by the standards of London's *ton*. But what she lacked in those areas—and in the false pride so fashionable of late—she made up in dignity and humanity. And all of this despite a lifetime of oppression and bad luck.

Birch nodded respectfully to his client. "Why not wait in

the carriage, m'lady. I would be happy to take care of the details here."

A small writing desk was being handed up and placed exactly where the slave woman had stood a moment earlier. Millicent watched several members of the crowd edge forward for a better look at the piece of furniture. They were far more interested in this item than in the human being who was auctioned off before it. Only the competition of the bidding had attracted their attention. She turned to watch the woman being led across the yard, with Sir Oliver trailing behind.

Appalled by the entire proceeding, Millicent pushed her way through the crowd to the carriage.

"She will be brought to my office this afternoon," Birch said as soon as he had climbed in some time later. "And, since you do not wish to have her delivered to your sister's home, I'll arrange for a place for her to stay until you're ready to leave for Melbury Hall."

"Thank you. We shall be leaving tomorrow morning," Millicent replied.

"Rest assured, m'lady, everything will be handled with the utmost discretion."

"I know it will," she said quietly, looking out the small window of the carriage at the door of the shed where the old woman had been taken. Millicent couldn't help but worry about how much more pain these horrible people would inflict on her before she was delivered to the lawyer's office that afternoon.

As they rode along in silence through the city, she thought

of the money she'd just spent. A hundred ten pounds was equivalent to seven months' worth of salaries of all twenty servants she employed at Melbury Hall, not counting the field hands. It was true that the purchase of the black woman would cut deeply into her rapidly diminishing funds. And she wasn't even considering the money that she needed to pay Jasper Hyde next month. Millicent rubbed her fingers over a dull ache in her temple and tried to think only of how much good it would do, bringing this woman back to Hertfordshire.

"Lady Wentworth," the lawyer said finally, breaking the silence as they drew near their destination, "we can't put off discussing your appointment with the Dowager Countess Aytoun any longer. I'm still completely in the dark concerning why we are going there."

"That makes two of us, Sir Oliver," she replied tiredly. "Her note summoning—or rather, inviting me—to meet with her arrived three days ago at Melbury Hall, and her groom stayed until I sent her an answer. I was to arrive at the Earl of Aytoun's town house in Hanover Square today at eleven this morning with my attorney. Nothing more was said."

"This sounds very abrupt. Do you know the countess?"

Millicent shook her head. "I do not. But then again, a year ago I didn't know Mr. Jasper Hyde, either. Nor the other half-dozen creditors who have endeavored to come after me from every quarter since Wentworth's death." She pulled the cloak tighter around herself. "One thing I've learned this past year and a half is that there is no hiding from those to whom my husband owed money. I have to face them—one by one—and try to make some reasonable arrangement to pay them back."

"You know that I admire you greatly in your efforts, but we both know you're encumbered almost beyond the point of recovery already." He paused. "You have some very generous friends, Lady Wentworth. If you would allow me to reveal to them just a hint of your hardship—"

"No, sir," she said sharply. "I find no shame in being poor. But I find great dishonor in begging. Please, I don't care to hear any more."

"As you wish, m'lady."

Millicent nodded gratefully at her lawyer. Sir Oliver had already served her well, and she trusted that he would honor her request.

"To set your mind a little at ease, though," he continued, "you should know that the Dowager Countess Aytoun is socially situated far differently than Mr. Hyde, or your late husband. She's a woman of great wealth, but she's rumored to be exceedingly...well, careful with her money. Some say she's so tightfisted that her own servants must struggle to receive their wages. In short, I cannot see her lending any money to Squire Wentworth."

"I'm relieved to hear that. I should have known that with your attention to detail we would not be walking into this meeting totally unprepared. What else have you learned about her?"

"A few things, m'lady. Lady Pennington's given name is Beatrice. She's been a widow for over five years. She's Scottish by birth, with the blood of Highlanders in her veins. She comes from an ancient family, and she married well besides."

"She has children?"

"Three sons. All men now. Lyon Pennington is the fourth Earl of Aytoun. The second son, Pierce Pennington, has apparently been making a fortune in the American colonies despite the embargo. And David Pennington, the youngest, is an officer in His Majesty's army. The countess herself led a very quiet life until the scandal that tore her family apart occurred this past summer."

"Scandal?"

Sir Oliver nodded. "Indeed, m'lady. It involved a young lady named Emma Douglas. I understand all three brothers were fond of her. She ended up marrying the oldest brother and became the countess of Aytoun two years ago."

That hardly sounded scandalous, but Millicent had no chance to ask any more questions as their carriage rolled to a stop in front of an elegant mansion facing Hanover Square. A footman in gold-trimmed livery greeted them as he opened the door of the carriage. Another servant escorted them up the wide marble steps to the front door.

Inside the mansion's entrance hall, yet another servant greeted them. As Millicent shed her cloak, her gaze took in the semicircular alcove at the far end of the hall and the ornate gilded scrolls and rosettes that decorated the high patterned ceiling. In a receiving area beyond an open set of doors, she could see upholstered furniture of deep walnut by Sheraton and Chippendale tastefully arranged about the room, while handsome carpets covered the brightly polished floors.

A tall, elderly steward approached and informed them that the dowager was waiting.

"What was the nature of the scandal?" she managed to whisper as they followed the steward and another servant up the sweeping circular stairs to a drawing room.

"Just rumors, m'lady," Birch whispered, "to the effect that the earl murdered his wife."

"But that is—"

She stopped as the door to the drawing room was opened. Trying to contain her shock and curiosity, Millicent entered as they were announced.

There were four people in the cozy, well-appointed room: the dowager countess, a pale gentleman standing by a desk that had a ledger book open on it, and two lady's maids.

Lady Aytoun was an older woman, obviously in ill health. She was sitting on a sofa with pillows propped behind her and a blanket on her lap. Blue eyes studied the visitors from behind a pair of spectacles.

Millicent gave a small curtsy. "Our apologies, my lady, for being delayed."

"Did you win the auction?" The dowager's abruptness caused Millicent to look over in surprise at Sir Oliver. He appeared as baffled as she was. "The African woman. Did you win the auction?"

"I...I did," she managed to get out. "But how did you know about it?"

"How much?"

Millicent bristled at the inquiry, but at the same time she felt no shame for what she'd done. "One hundred ten pounds. Though I must tell you I don't know what business it is of—"

"Add it to the tally, Sir Richard." The dowager waved a

hand at the gentleman still standing by the desk. "A worthy cause."

Sir Oliver stepped forward. "May I say, m'lady—"

"Pray, save the idle prattle, young man. Come and sit. Both of you."

Millicent's lawyer, who probably hadn't been addressed as "young man" in decades, stared openmouthed for a moment. Then, as he and Millicent did as they were instructed, the countess dismissed the servants with a wave of her hand.

"Very well. I know both of you, and you know me. That pasty-faced bag of bones over there is my lawyer, Sir Richard Maitland." The old woman arched an eyebrow in the direction of her attorney, who bowed stiffly and sat. "And now, the reason why I invited you here."

Millicent could not even hazard a guess as to what was coming next.

"People acting on my behalf have been reporting to me about you for some time now, Lady Wentworth. You have surpassed my expectations." Lady Aytoun removed her spectacles. "No reason for dallying. You're here because I have a business proposition."

"A business proposition?" Millicent murmured.

"Indeed. I want you to marry my son, the Earl of Aytoun. By a special license. Today."

Read more of ***Borrowed Dreams***

ABOUT THE AUTHOR

USA Today Bestselling Authors Nikoo and Jim McGoldrick have crafted over fifty fast-paced, conflict-filled novels, along with two works of nonfiction, under the pseudonyms May McGoldrick, Jan Coffey, and Nik James.

These popular and prolific authors write historical romance, suspense, mystery, historical Westerns, and young adult novels. They are four-time Rita Award Finalists and the winners of numerous awards for their writing, including the Daphne DeMaurier Award for Excellence, the *Romantic Times Magazine* Reviewers' Choice Award, three NJRW Golden Leaf Awards, two Holt Medallions, and the Connecticut Press Club Award for Best Fiction. Their work is included in the Popular Culture Library collection of the National Museum of Scotland.

facebook.com/MayMcGoldrick

twitter.com/MayMcGoldrick

instagram.com/maymcgoldrick

bookbub.com/authors/may-mcgoldrick